Dad & Mother
From
Billy & Dan

America the Beautiful in the Words of
HENRY DAVID
THOREAU

Thoreau found in the solitude of nature a source of abundance, a place to think and reflect, a subject for writing.

America the Beautiful
In the Words of
HENRY DAVID THOREAU

By the Editors of COUNTRY BEAUTIFUL

Editorial Direction: Michael P. Dineen
Edited by Robert L. Polley

Published by Country Beautiful Corporation, Waukesha, Wisconsin

PHOTO CREDITS

Gene Ahrens, 50-51, 58, 59 (top), 84 (top), 87, 88-89, 97; Frank Aleksandrowicz, 48; J. W. Ambler from National Audubon Society, 62-63 (bottom); James Fehring, 53; Charles R. Fowler, 33, 34-35 (top), 59 (bottom), 90; Freelance Photographers Guild, 28-29, 38-39 (top); John H. Gerard from National Audubon Society, 63 (top), 65; Olive Glasgow, 91, 94; Woodrow Goodpaster from National Audubon Society, 62 (top); Martin Hanson, 80; Grant Heilman, 4, 11, 12, 14-15, 16, 19, 20, 21, 22, 26, 27, 31, 32, 36, 39 (bottom), 45, 47, 49, 54, 56-57, 61, 64, 69, 70, 73, 76, 83, 84-85 (top right), 84-85 (bottom right), 86, 95, 96, 98; R. Mandle, 55; Phil McCafferty, 25, 35 (bottom), 92-93; David Muench, 13, 40-41, 70, 74, 77, 79, 81; National Park Service, 44; The New York Public Library Picture Collection, 9; C. J. Ott from National Audubon Society, 66; Madeline Tourtelot, 43.

Country Beautiful Corporation is a wholly owned subsidiary of Flick-Reedy Corporation: President: Frank Flick; Vice President and General Manager: Michael P. Dineen; Treasurer and Secretary: August Caamano.

Copyright © MCMLXVI by Country Beautiful Corporation. All rights reserved. No portion of this book may be reproduced in any form whatsoever without written permission. Library of Congress Catalog Card Number 66-12998. Printed in the U.S.A. Book design by Robert Fehring. Color separations by Mueller Color Plate Company. This edition published by Country Beautiful Corporation.

CONTENTS

Introduction 8

    I   THE FOUR SEASONS • *11*

   II   LANDSCAPE AND WATERSCAPE • *29*

  III   PHENOMENA OF NATURE • *41*

  IV   FOCUSING DOWN ON NATURE • *51*

   V   A NEST OF BIRDS • *63*

  VI   OF TIME AND MAN • *73*

 VII   THE NATURE OF MAN AND NATURE • *85*

INTRODUCTION

There can be little doubt that the past century has brought us to a greater understanding and appreciation of the thoughts, attitudes and vision of Henry David Thoreau, naturalist, essayist, social critic, poet. Thoreau's concept of non-violent civil disobedience when normal legislative and judicial channels are closed to dissent has never seemed more relevant to the American conscience than it does today. His belief that "the mass of men lead lives of quiet desperation" foreshadows one of the dominating maladies of our Age of Anxiety. Thoreau's concern for bringing man into harmony with his environment speaks directly to today's problems of urban sprawl, air and water pollution, automation, conservation, and burgeoning leisure time. In short, Thoreau, while rambling through the fields near his beloved Concord, seems to have probed the soul of modern man with a deliberation and insight few men since can equal.

Thoreau's wisdom gains its impact through the strength and clarity of his writing. He was not a scholar or a philosopher in any strict sense. He was a writer and author, one of the great prose stylists of the American language. His economy of style and his ability to create memorable phrases is worthy of the classical Greek authors whom Thoreau loved and fluently read in their own language. The quality of his poetry is more controversial. Some recent critics have described it disparagingly as "scholarly doggerel," others consider it to have been in advance of its time, reflecting the English metaphysical poets and anticipatory to the later poetry of Emily Dickinson.

Thoreau was born in Concord of an intelligent family with few financial resources. At some sacrifice he was sent to Concord Academy and Harvard where he was an honor student. Through the influence of men such as Orestes Brownson, the famous Unitarian minister with whom Thoreau boarded for a short time, he learned to read German, Latin and Greek. He also knew Italian, French and, to a lesser extent, Spanish. His reading of Coleridge, Carlyle and the Hindu scriptures contributed to the development of his ideas.

In 1841 Thoreau went to live at the home of Ralph Waldo Emerson in Concord, beginning a friendship that lasted through some later periods of estrangement to the end of his life. In 1845 Thoreau built a cabin on some land owned by Emerson in the woods beside Walden Pond because, he later wrote, "I wished to live deliberately, to front only the essential facts of life, and see if I could learn what it had to teach." He lived there two years, removed from the village, but not as a hermit. He went into Concord almost every day and passers-by visited him in his cabin from time to time.

Thoreau had been deeply interested in nature since childhood and his Walden experience only emphasizes the fact that his observations of and thoughts about nature were closely related to his beliefs about man and society. Because he realized the need of man for the natural world no other writer has treasured the gifts of the American land as did he.

HENRY DAVID THOREAU (1817-1862)

During his second summer at Walden, Thoreau was jailed for not paying his poll tax. He hadn't paid his tax for several years because he had decided that he could not support a government which implicitly sanctioned slavery. He was insensed when his aunt paid the tax and secured his release. Soon after, he gave his famous lecture on "Resistance to Civil Government." Its written version was read by Gandhi in jail many decades later and became the basis for his passive-resistance campaign to free India and later played a substantial part in the American Negroes' civil rights movement.

After leaving Walden Thoreau earned a living as a mason, painter, carpenter and day-laborer. The latter he found the "most independent" of any occupation. He became one of the best surveyors in Concord and he invented a process which helped his family's pencil factory. Relatively little of Thoreau's writing was published during his lifetime, although he had a modest reputation as a lecturer and author. Only *Walden* achieved any success in sales. He died in 1862 not long after a visit to Minnesota, which was as close as he ever got to the West he often wrote about.

In the Jeffersonian tradition Thoreau believed "that state is best which governs least" but he had no systematic philosophy and he certainly was not an anarchist or revolutionist. He was that rare person, a genuine individualist who never suggested that his way was the best way for everyone to live. He simply believed men's lives more important than the state and the state had to be resisted when it threatened individual integrity. Thoreau gave this belief such vivid expression in his life and his writings that even those who disagree with him have to admit that his belief has become a vital tenet of the American tradition.

— ROBERT L. POLLEY

Is beauty tangible? A quick answer would be, "Yes, it's tangible." But there is more. You know, when you get past 50 you may get to reminiscing about what you have done, what you remember, what was really worthwhile.

What surfaces with me? What do I remember? Little pictures like this, a beautiful oasis in my life: Three or four days in a summer that my husband and our two children spent with another couple and their four children on a sandy, rather quiet beach — walking along with the sand coming up between your toes, watching the wind in the reeds along the sand dunes. Just sitting with the glorious rhythm of the waves coming in can be the most relaxing thing in the world.

These were days that are worth very much to me, but I suppose it is perhaps in an intangible way.

We live in a country founded, in part, by a man who was daring enough to say that we were devoted to life, liberty and the pursuit of happiness — he ranked the pursuit of happiness right up there at the top. And beauty and happiness are certainly inextricably tied together.

Mrs. Lyndon B. Johnson
Excerpt from interview in
U.S. News & World Report, Feb. 22, 1965

I
THE FOUR SEASONS

Even before the earliest green the thaw and gurgle of the woodland stream evidences the coming of spring.

Still cold and blustering.... How silent are the footsteps of spring! There, too, where there is a fraction of the meadow, two rods over, quite bare, under the bank, in this warm recess at the head of the meadow, though the rest of the meadow is covered with snow a foot or more in depth, I am surprised to see the skunk-cabbage, with its great spear-heads open and ready to blossom.... The spring advances in spite of snow and ice, and cold even.

JOURNAL, March 30, 1856

Early in May, the oaks, hickories, maples, and other trees, just putting out amidst the pine woods around the pond, imparted a brightness like sunshine to the landscape, especially in cloudy days, as if the sun were breaking through mists and shining faintly on the hill-sides here and there.

From WALDEN

This is the first really spring day.... The sound of distant crows and cocks is full of spring.... Something analogous to the thawing of the ice seems to have taken place in the air. At the end of winter there is a season in which we are daily expecting spring, and finally a day when it arrives.... Methinks the first obvious evidence of spring is the pushing out of the swamp willow catkins... then the pushing up of skunk-cabbage spathes (and pads at the bottom of water).

JOURNAL, March 10, 1853

... We had the mountain in sight before us,—its sublime gray mass.... Probably these crests of the earth are for the most part of one color in all lands, that gray color of antiquity which nature loves; color of unpainted wood, weather-stain, time-stain; not glaring nor gaudy; the color of all roofs, the color of all things that endure, the color that wears well; color of Egyptians ruins, of mummies and all antiquity: baked in the sun... that hard, enduring gray; a terrene sky-color; solidified air with a tinge of earth.

JOURNAL, June 2, 1858

Our voices sound differently and betray the spring. . . . These earliest spring days are peculiarly pleasant. We shall have no more of them for a year. I am apt to forget that we may have raw and blustering days a month hence. The combination of this delicious air, which you do not want to be warmer or softer, with the presence of ice and snow, you sitting on the bare russet portions, the south hillsides, of the earth, this is the charm of these days. It is the summer beginning to show itself like an old friend in the midst of winter. You ramble from one drier russet patch to another. These are your stages. You have the air and sun of summer, over snow and ice, and in some places even the rustling of dry leaves under your feet, as in Indian-summer days.

JOURNAL, March 10, 1859

The eternal mountain and its eternal gray intrigued Thoreau. Here, clouds rest on Bailey Range and Elva Valley at Olympic National Park, Washington.

Come, let's roam the breezy pastures...

THE BREEZE'S INVITATION

Come, let's roam the breezy pastures,
Where the freest zephyrs blow,
Batten on the oak tree's rustle,
And the pleasant insect bustle,
Dripping with the streamlet's flow.

What if I no wings do wear,
Thro' this solid seeming air
I can skim like any swallow
Who so dareth let her follow,
And we'll be a jovial pair.

Like two careless swifts let's sail,
Zephyrus shall think for me—
Over hill and over dale,
Riding on the easy gale,
We will scan the earth and sea.

Yonder see that willow tree
Winnowing the buxom air,
You a gnat and I a bee,
With our merry minstrelsy
We will make a concert there.

One green leaf shall be our screen,
Till the sun doth go to bed,
I the king and you the queen
Of that peaceful little green,
Without any subject's aid.

To our music Time will linger,
And earth open wide her ear,
Nor shall any need to tarry
To immortal verse to marry
Such sweet music as he'll hear.

Light winds meander through summer fields and meadows buffeting flocks of sheep while they graze.

At the beginning of day mists soften the land and trees and give them a unique character.

I was reminded, this morning before I rose, of those undescribed ambrosial mornings of summer which I can remember, when a thousand birds were heard gently twittering and ushering in the light, like the argument to a new canto of an epic and heroic poem. The serenity, the infinite promise, of such a morning! The song or twitter of birds drips from the leaves like dew. Then there was something divine and immortal in our life, when I have waked up on my couch in the woods and seen the day dawning, and heard the twittering of the birds.

JOURNAL, March 10, 1852

Morning's haze, serene and kind...

This is emphatically one of the dog-days. A dense fog . . . and the clouds (which did not let in any sun all day) were the dog-day fog and mist, which threatened no rain. A muggy but comfortable day.

As we go along the corner road, the dense fog for a background relieves pleasantly the outlines of every tree . . . so that each is seen as a new object. . . .

JOURNAL, July 31, 1859

This is June, the month of grass and leaves. The deciduous trees are investing the evergreens and revealing how dark they are. Already the aspens are trembling again, and a new summer is offered me. I feel a little fluttered in my thoughts, as if I might be too late. Each season is but an infinitesimal point. It no sooner comes than it is gone. It has no duration. It simply gives a tone and hue to my thought. Each annual phenomenon is a reminiscence and prompting. Our thoughts and sentiments answer to the revolutions of the seasons, as two cog-wheels fit into each other. We are conversant with only one point of contact at a time, from which we receive a prompting and impulse and instantly pass to a new season or point of contact. A year is made up of a certain series and number of sensations and thoughts which have their language in nature. Now I am ice, now I am sorrel. Each experience reduces itself to a mood of the mind.

JOURNAL, June 6, 1857

Another hot day 96° at mid-afternoon. . . . The elm avenue above the Wheeler farm is one of the hottest places in the town; the heat is reflected from the dusty wood. The grass by the roadside begins to have a dry, dusty look. The melted ice is running almost in a stream from the countryman's covered wagon, containing butter, which is to be conveyed hard to Boston market.

JOURNAL, July 12, 1859

The aged year turns on its couch of leaves...

I MARK THE SUMMER'S SWIFT DECLINE

I mark the summer's swift decline
The springing sward its grave clothes weaves
Whose rustling woods the gales confine
The aged year turns on its couch of leaves.

Oh, could I catch the sounds remote
Could I but tell to human ear —
The strains which on the breezes float
And sing the requiem of the dying year.

Fall, with its colorful trees
under blue skies and cool air, is still
the annual wonderment of man.

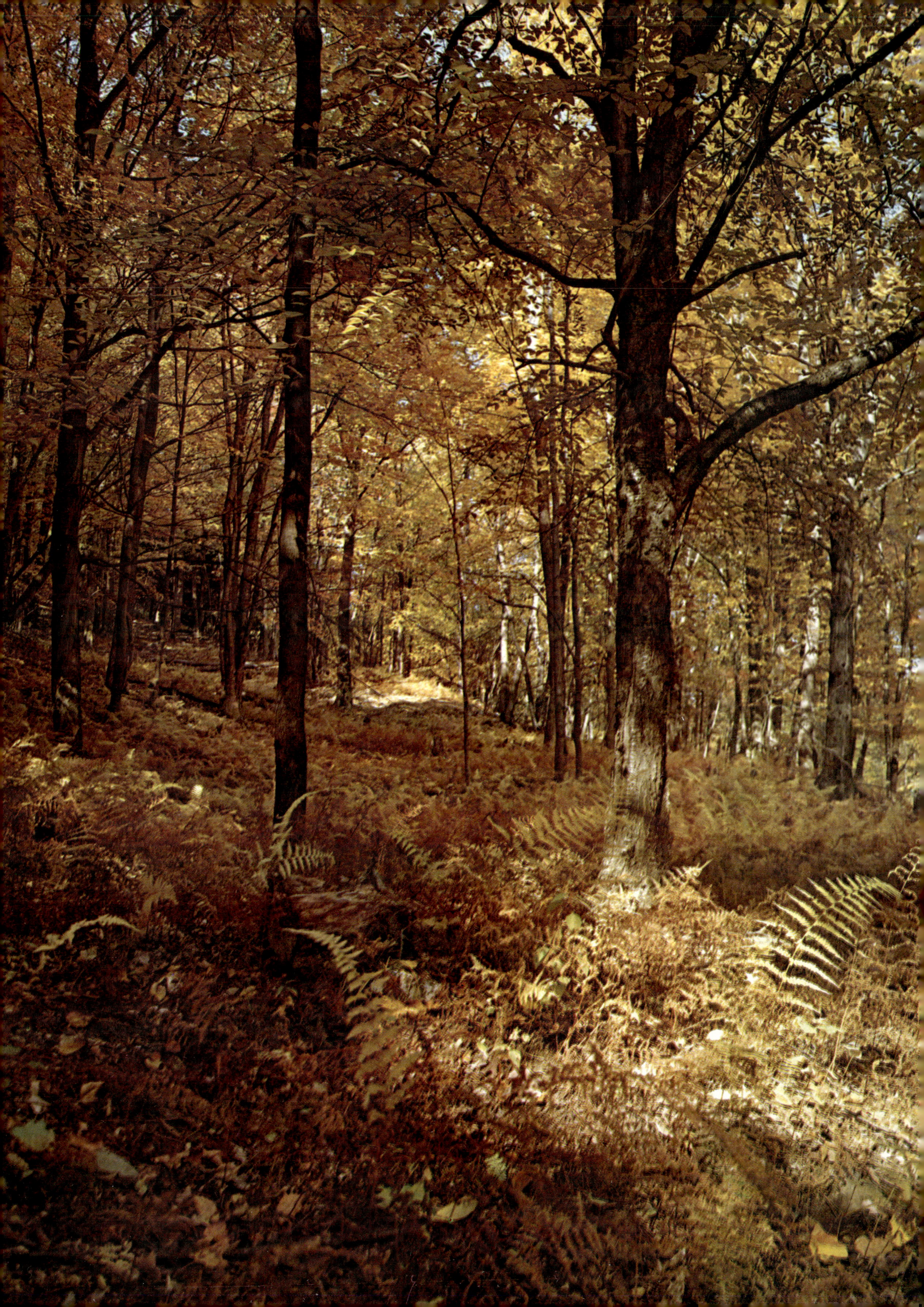

Color stands for all ripeness and success...

A bumble bee on a peach blossom is a common sight in late summer and fall.

The river is very nearly down to summer level now, and I notice there, among other phenomena of low water . . . the great yellow lily pads flat on bare mud. . . .

JOURNAL, July 28, 1859

The large buds, suddenly pushing out late in the spring from dry sticks which had seemed to be dead, developed themselves as by magic into graceful green and tender boughs, an inch in diameter; and sometimes as I sat at my window, so heedlessly did they grow and tax their weak joints, I heard a fresh and tender bough suddenly fall like a fan to the ground, when there was not a breath of air stirring, broken off by its own weight. In August, the large masses of berries, which, when in flower, had attracted many wild bees, gradually assumed their bright velvety crimson hue, and by their weight again bent down and broke the tender limbs.

From WALDEN

Some single red maples are very splendid now, the whole tree bright-scarlet against the cold green pines; now when very few trees are changed, a most remarkable object in the landscape; seen a mile off. It is too fair to be believed, especially seen against the light. Some are a reddish or else greenish yellow, others with red or yellow cheeks. I suspect that the yellow maples had not scarlet blossoms.

JOURNAL, September 26, 1854

The brilliant autumnal colors are red and yellow and the various tints, hues, and shades of these. Blue is reserved to be the color of the sky, but yellow and red are the colors of the earth-flower. Every fruit, on ripening, and just before its fall, acquires a bright tint. So do the leaves; so the sky before the end of the day, and the year near its setting. October is the red sunset sky, November the later twilight. Color stands for all ripeness and success. We have dreamed that the hero should carry his color aloft, as a symbol of the ripeness of his virtue. The noblest feature, the eye, is the fairest-colored, the jewel of the body. The warrior's flag is the flower which precedes his fruit.

JOURNAL, October 24, 1858

In early fall the varying times of autumnal change present contrasts of green and red.

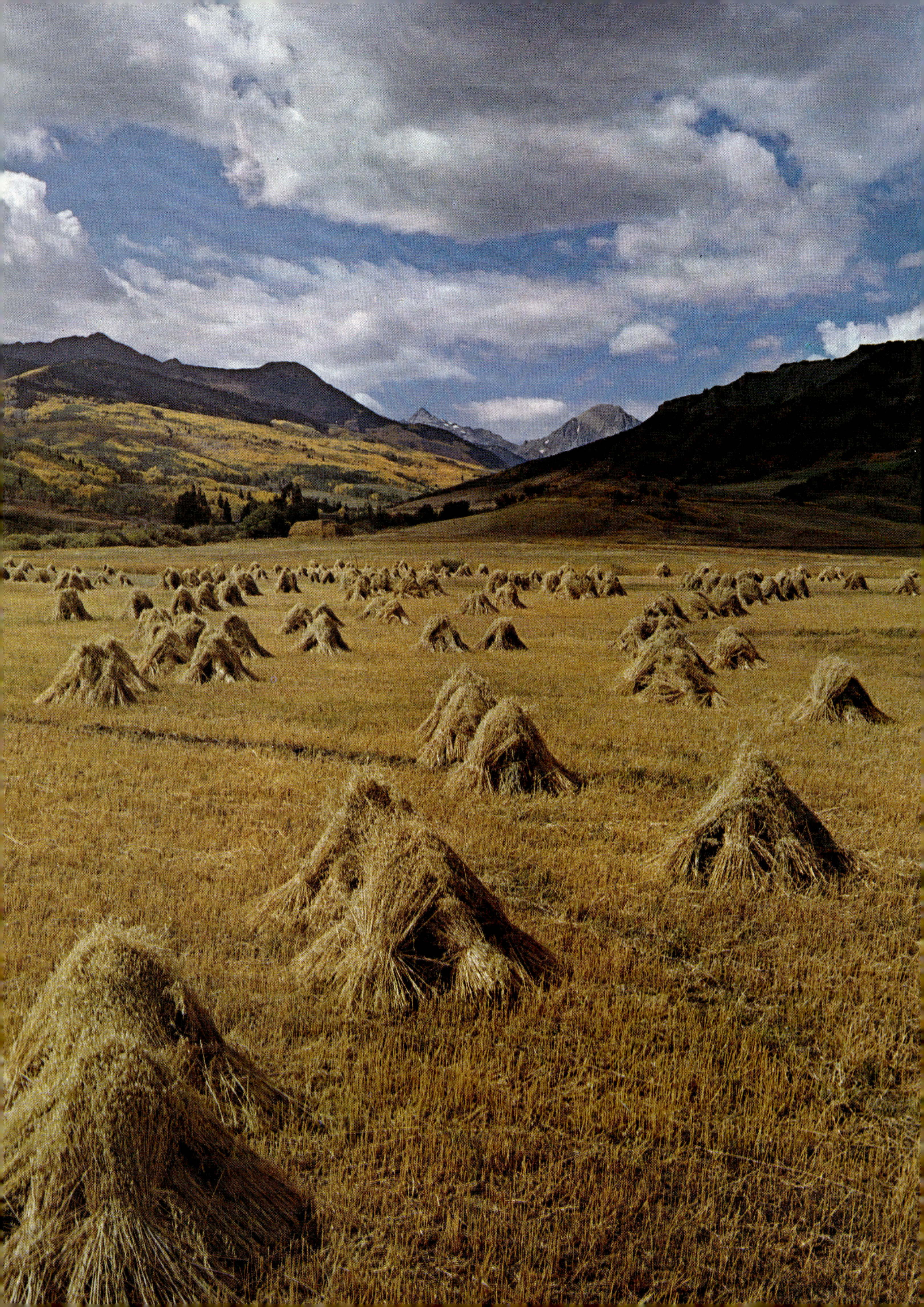

*The fineness of October airs
upon fields lit by the harvest sun...*

ON FIELDS O'ER WHICH THE REAPER'S HAND HAS PASSED

On fields o'er which the reaper's hand has passed,
Lit by the harvest moon and autumn sun,
My thoughts like stubble floating in the wind
And of such fineness as October airs,
There after harvest could I glean my life
A richer harvest reaping without toil,
And weaving gorgeous fancies at my will,
In subtler webs than finest summer haze.

Stacks of bundled hay line
a Colorado pasture after the harvest.

Another perfect Indian-summer day. Some small bushy white asters still survive.

The autumnal tints grow gradually darker and duller, but not less rich to my eye. And now a hillside near the river exhibits the darkest, crispy reds and browns of every hue, all agreeably blended. At the foot, next the meadow, stands a front rank of smoke-like maples bare of leaves, intermixed with yellow birches. Higher up, are red oaks of various shades of dull red, with yellowish, perhaps black oaks intermixed, and walnuts, now brown, and near the hilltop, or rising above the rest, perhaps, a still yellow oak, and here and there amid the rest or in the foreground on the meadow, dull ashy salmon-colored white oaks large and small, all these contrasting with the clear liquid, sempiternal green of pines.

JOURNAL, October 25, 1852

It is wonderful what gradation and harmony there is in nature. The light reflected from bare twigs at this season . . . is not only like that from gossamer, but like that which will ere long be reflected from the ice that will incrust them. So the bleached herbage of the fields is like frost, and frost like snow, and one prepares for the other.

JOURNAL, November 13, 1858

Perhaps what most moves us in winter is some reminiscence of far-off summer. . . . What beauty in the running brooks! What life! What society! The cold is merely superficial: it is summer still at the core, far, far within. It is in the cawing of the crow, the crowning of the cock, the warmth of the sun on our backs. I hear faintly the cawing of a crow far, far away, echoing from some unseen wood-side, as if deadened by the springlike vapor which the sun is drawing from the ground. It mingles with the slight murmur of the village, the sound of children at play, as one stream empties gently into another, and the wild and tame are one. What a delicious sound! It is not merely crow calling to crow, for it speaks to me too. I am part of one great creature with him; if he has voice, I have ears. I can hear when he calls, and have engaged not to shoot nor stone him if he will caw to me each spring.

JOURNAL, January 12, 1855

The harmony in nature is evident in late autumn sunsets viewed through leafless branches.

These are true mornings of creation, original and poetic days, not mere repetitions of the past. There is no lingering of yesterday's fogs, only such a mist as might have adorned the first morning.

JOURNAL, January 6, 1858

Every part of nature teaches that the passing away of one life is the making room for another. The oak dies down to the ground, leaving within its rind a rich virgin mould, which will impart a vigorous life to an infant forest. The pine leaves a sandy and sterile soil, the harder woods a strong and fruitful mould.

So this constant abrasion and decay makes the soil of our future growth. As I live now so shall I reap. If I grow pines and birches, my virgin mould will not sustain the oak; but pines and birches, or, perchance, weeds and brambles, will constitute my second growth.

JOURNAL, October 24, 1837

Put the seal of silence now upon the leaves beneath...

WINTER MEMORIES

Within the circuit of this plodding life
There enter moments of an azure hue,
Untarnished fair as is the violet
Or anemone, when the spring strews them
By some meandering rivulet, which make
the best philosophy untrue that aims
But to console man for his grievances.
I have remembered when the winter came,
High in my chamber in the frosty nights,
When in the still light of the cheerful moon,
On every twig and rail and jutting spout,
The icy spears were adding to their length
Against the arrows of the coming sun,
How in the shimmering noon of summer past
Some unrecorded beam slanted across
The upland pastures where the Johnswort grew;
Or heard, amid the verdure of my mind,
The bee's long smothered hum, on the blue flag
Loitering amidst the mead; or busy rill,
Which now through all its course stands still and dumb
Its own memorial,—purling at its play
Along the slopes, and through the meadows next,
Until its youthful sound was hushed at last
In the staid current of the lowland stream;
Or seen the furrows shine but late upturned,
And where the fieldfare followed in the rear,
When all the fields around lay bound and hoar
Beneath a thick integument of snow.
So by God's cheap economy made rich
To go upon my winter's task again.

The pine trees endure a lonely quiet while covered with snow during the long winter months.

From WHEN WINTER FRINGES EVERY BOUGH

When Winter fringes every bough
   With his fantastic wreath,
And puts the seal of silence now
   Upon the leaves beneath;

When every stream in its pent-house
   Goes gurgling on its way,
And in his gallery the mouse
   Nibbleth the meadow hay;

Methinks the summer still is nigh,
   And lurketh underneath,
As that same meadow mouse doth lie
   Snug in the last year's heath.

Most of nature, its plants and its rivers and streams, lies dormant during winter under a constantly renewed snow.

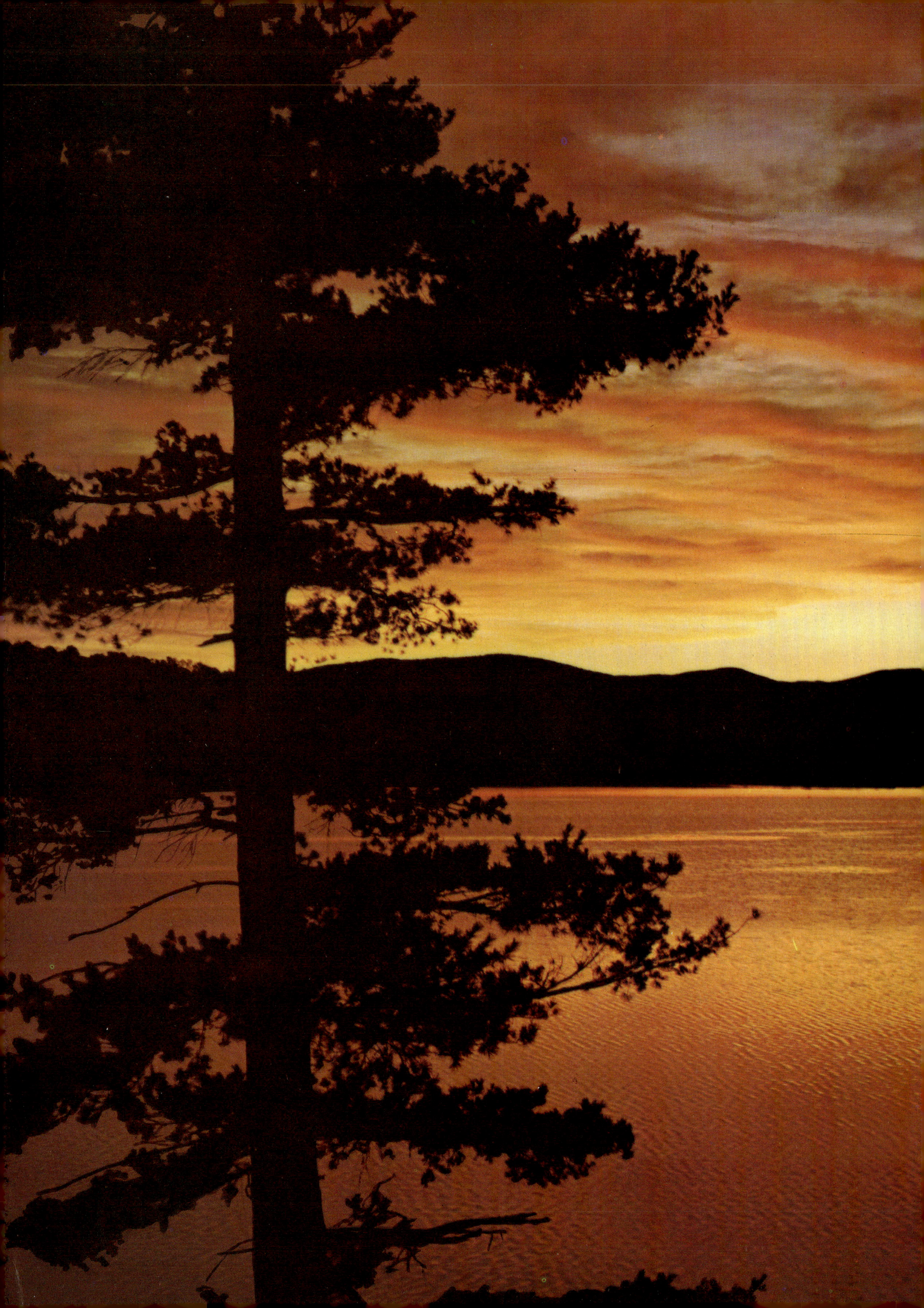

II
LANDSCAPE AND WATERSCAPE

The landscape looked clean and pure...

I perceive the spring in the softened air. . . . Apparently in consequence of the very warm sun . . . falling on the earth four-fifths covered with snow and ice, there is an almost invisible vapor held in suspension. . . . Looking through this transparent vapor, all surfaces, not osiers and open water alone, look more vivid. The hardness of winter is relaxed.

There is a fine effluence surrounding the wood, as if the sap had begun to stir and you could detect it a mile off. Such is the difference between an object seen through a warm, moist, and soft air and a cold, dry, hard one. Such is the genialness of nature that the trees appear to have put out feelers by which the senses apprehend them more tenderly. I do not know that the woods are ever more beautiful, or affect me more.

JOURNAL, March 10, 1859

How charming the contrast of land and water, especially a temporary island in the flood, with its new and tender shores of waving outline, so withdrawn yet habitable, above all if it rises into a hill high above the water and contrasting with it the more, and if that hill is wooded, suggesting wilderness! Our vernal lakes have a beauty to my mind which they would not possess if they were more permanent. Everything is in rapid flux here, suggesting that Nature is alive to her extremities and superficies. . . . But this particular phase of beauty is fleeting. Nature has so many shows for us she cannot afford to give much time to this.

JOURNAL, March 28, 1859

Above me the cloudless blue sky; beneath, the . . . sky-reflecting ice . . At a distance in several directions I see the tawny earth streaked or spotted with white where the bank or hills and fields appear, or else the green-black evergreen forests, or the brown, or russet, or tawny deciduous woods, and here and there, where the agitated surface of the river is exposed, the blue-black water. That dark-eyed water, especially where I see it at right angles with the direction of the sun, is it not the first sign of spring? How its darkness contrasts with the general lightness of the winter! It has more life in it than any part of the earth's surface. It is where one of the arteries of the earth is palpable, visible.

JOURNAL, February 12, 1860

The winding river and the surrounding landscape contrast with each other to bring a heightened beauty to both.

The landscape looked singularly clean and pure and dry, the air, like a pure glass, being laid over the picture, the trees so tidy, and stripped of their leaves; the meadows and pastures, clothed with clean dry grass, looked as if they had been swept; ice on the water and winter in the air; but yet not a particle of snow on the ground. The woods, divested in great part of their leaves, are being ventilated. It is the season of perfect works, of hard, tough, ripe twigs, not of tender buds and leaves. The leaves have made their wood, and a myriad new withes stand up all around pointing to the sky, able to survive the cold. It is only the perennial that you see, the iron age of the year.

JOURNAL, November 25, 1850

Thoreau felt that lakes should be named for the animals in or near it, such as White Heron Lake in Pennsylvania.

Flint's Pond! Such is the poverty of our nomenclature. What right had the unclean and stupid farmer, whose farm abutted on this sky water, whose shores he had ruthlessly laid bare, to give his name to it? Some skin-flint, who loved better the reflecting surface of a dollar, or a bright cent, in which he could see his own brazen face; who regarded even the wild ducks which settled in it as trespassers; his fingers grown into crooked and horny talons from the long habit of grasping harpy-like;— so it is not named for me. I go not there to see him nor to hear of him; who never *saw* it, who never bathed in it, who never loved it, who never protected it, who never spoke a good word for it, nor thanked God that He had made it. Rather let it be named from the fishes that swim in it, the wild fowl or quadrupeds which frequent it, the wild flowers which grow by its shores, or some wild man or child the thread of whose history is interwoven with its own; not from him who could show no title to it but the deed which a like-minded neighbor or legislature gave him,— him who thought only of its money value; whose present perchance cursed all the shore; who exhausted the land around it, and would fain have exhausted the waters within it; who regretted only that it was not English hay or cranberry meadow, —there was nothing to redeem it, forsooth, in his eyes,—and would have drained and sold it for the mud at its bottom. It did not turn his mill, and it was no privilege to him to behold it. I respect not his labors, his farm where everything has its price, who would carry the landscape, who would carry his God, to market, if he could get anything for him; who goes to market *for* his god as it is; on whose farm nothing grows free, whose fields bear no crops, whose meadows no flowers, whose trees no fruit, but dollars; who loves not the beauty of his fruits, whose fruits are not ripe for him till they are turned to dollars. Give me the poverty that enjoys true wealth.

From WALDEN

I want to go soon and live away by the pond, where I shall hear only the wind whispering among the reeds. It will be success if I shall have left myself behind. But my friends ask what I will do when I get there. Will it not be employment enough to watch the progress of the seasons?

JOURNAL, December 24, 1841

For the first week, whenever I look out on the pond it impressed me like a tarn high up on the side of a mountain, its bottom far above the surface of other lakes, and, as the sun rose, I saw it throwing off its nightly clothing of mist, and here and there, by degrees, its soft ripples or its smooth reflecting surface was revealed, while the mists, like ghosts, were stealthily withdrawing in every direction into the woods, as at the breaking up of some nocturnal conventicle. The very dew seemed to hang upon the trees later into the day than usual, as on the sides of mountains.

From WALDEN

And the water-lily floats on the smooth surface of slow waters, amid rounded shields of leaves, bucklers, red beneath, which simulate a green field, perfuming the air. Each instantly the prey of the spoiler,—the rose-bug and water-insects. How transitory the perfect beauty of the rose and the lily! The highest, intensest color belongs to the land, the purest, perchance, to the water. The lily is perhaps the only flower which all are eager to pluck; it may be partly because of its inaccessibility to most.

JOURNAL, June 26, 1852

Walden Pond, located near Concord, Massachusetts, where Thoreau spent much time, as it appears today.

The river's gentle flow...

Concord River is remarkable for the gentleness of its current, which is scarcely perceptible, and some have referred to its influence the proverbial moderation of the inhabitants of Concord, as exhibited in the Revolution, and on later occasions. It has been proposed that the town should adopt for its coat of arms a field verdant, with the Concord circling nine times round. I have read that a descent of an eighth of an inch in a mile is sufficient to produce a flow. Our river has, probably, very near the smallest allowance. The story is current, at any rate, though I believe that strict history will not bear it out, that the only bridge ever carried away on the main branch, within the limits of the town, was driven up stream by the wind. But wherever it makes a sudden bend it is shallower and swifter, and asserts its title to be called a river. Compared with the other tributaries of the Merrimack, it appears to have been properly named Musketaquid, or Meadow River, by the Indians. For the most part, it creeps through broad meadows, adorned with scattered oaks, where the cranberry is found in abundance, covering the ground like a mossbed. A row of sunken dwarf willows borders the stream on one or both sides, while at a greater distance the meadow is skirted with maples, alders, and other fluviatile trees, overrun with the grape vine, which bears fruit in its season, purple, red, white, and other grapes. Still further from the stream, on the edge of the firm land, are seen the gray and white dwellings of the inhabitants. According to the valuation of 1831, there were in Concord two thousand one hundred and eleven acres, or about one-seventh of the whole territory, in meadow; this standing next in the list after pasturage and unimproved lands, and, judging from the returns of previous years, the meadow is not reclaimed so fast as the woods are cleared.

The sluggish artery of the Concord meadows steals thus unobserved through the town, without a murmur or a pulsebeat, its general course from south-west to north-east, and its length about fifty miles; a huge volume of matter, ceaselessly rolling through the plains and valleys of the substantial earth, with the moccasined tred of an Indian warrior, making haste from the high places of the earth to its ancient reservoir.

From A WEEK ON THE CONCORD
AND MERRIMACK RIVERS

The Concord River, from the North Bridge, where the Battle of Concord was fought in 1775.

It is impossible to remember a week ago. A river of Lethe flows with many windings the year through, separating one season from another. The heavens for a few days have been lost. It has been a sort of paradise instead. As with the seashore, so it is with the universal earth-shore, not in summer can you look far into the ocean of the ether. They who come to this world as to a watering-place in the summer for coolness and luxury never get the far and fine November views of heaven. Is not all the summer akin to a paradise? We have to bathe in ponds to brace ourselves. The earth is blue now,—the near hills, in this haze.

JOURNAL, May 9, 1852

Ice-breaks in spring have a sound of promise because they bring the needed food for the next season's crop.

In the brooks the slight grating sound of small cakes of ice, floating with various speed, is full of content and promise, and where the water gurgles under a natural bridge, you may hear these hasty rafts hold conversation in an undertone. Every rill is a channel for the juices of the meadow. Last year's grasses and flower-stalks have been steeped in rain and snow, and now the brooks flow with meadow tea,—thoroughwort, mint, flag-root, and pennyroyal, all at one draught.

JOURNAL, March 8, 1840

The sea-shore is naked nature...

All the morning we had heard the sea roar on the eastern shore, which was several miles distant . . . though a school-boy, whom we overtook, hardly knew what we meant, his ears were so used to it. He would have more plainly heard the same sound in a shell. It was a very inspiring sound to walk by, filling the whole air, that of the sea dashing against the land, heard several miles inland. Instead of having a dog to growl before your door, to have an Atlantic Ocean to growl for a whole Cape! On the whole, we were glad of the storm, which would show us the ocean in its angriest mood.

From CAPE COD

Whitecaps rush upon the rocky coast of northern New England slowly wearing down the formidable shore line.

The most foreign and picturesque structures on the Cape, to an inlander, not excepting the salt-works, are the wind-mills, — gray-looking octagonal towers, with long timbers slanting to the ground in the rear, and there resting on a cart-wheel, by which their fans are turned round to face the wind. These appeared also to serve in some measure for props against its force.

From CAPE COD

The white breakers were rushing to the shore; the foam ran up the sand, and then ran back as far as we could see (and we imagined how much farther along the Atlantic coast, before and behind us), as regularly, to compare great things with small, as the master of a choir beats time with his white wand; and ever and anon a higher wave caused us hastily to deviate from our path, and we looked back on our tracks filled with water and foam. The breakers looked like droves of a thousand wild horses of Neptune, rushing to the shore, with their white manes streaming far behind; and when at length the sun shone for a moment, their manes were rainbow-tinted. Also, the long kelp-weed was tossed up from time to time, like the tails of sea-cows sporting in the brine.

From CAPE COD

The sea-shore is a sort of neutral ground, a most advantageous point from which to contemplate this world. It is even a trivial place. The waves forever rolling to the land are too far-travelled and untamable to be familiar. Creeping along the endless beach amid the sun-squall and the foam, it occurs to us that we, too, are the product of sea-slime.

It is a wild, rank place, and there is no flattery in it. Strewn with crabs, horse-shoes, and razor-clams, and whatever the sea casts up, — a vast *morgue,* where famished dogs may range in packs, and crows come daily to glean the pittance which the tide leaves them. The carcasses of men and beasts together lie stately up upon its shelf, rotting and bleaching in the sun and waves, and each tide turns them in their beds, and tucks fresh sand under them. There is naked Nature, inhumanly sincere, wasting no thought on man, nibbling at the cliffy shore where gulls wheel amid the spray.

From CAPE COD

*Every day
a new picture
is painted...*

We found ourselves at once on an apparently boundless plain, without a tree or a fence, or, with one or two exceptions, a house in sight. Instead of fences, the earth was sometimes thrown up into a slight ridge. My companion compared it to the rolling prairies of Illinois. In the storm of wind and rain which raged when we traversed it, it no doubt appeared more vast and desolate than it really is. As there were no hills, but only here and there a dry hollow in the midst of the waste, and the distant horizon was concealed by mist, we did not know whether it was high or low. A solitary traveller whom we saw perambulating in the distance loomed like a giant. He appeared to walk slouchingly, as if held up from above by straps under his shoulders, as much as supported by the plain below. Men and boys would have appeared alike at a little distance, there being no object by which to measure them. Indeed, to an inlander, the Cape landscape is a constant mirage. This kind of country extended a mile or two each way. These were the "Plains of Nauset," once covered with wood, where in winter the winds howl and the snow blows right merrily in the face of the traveller. I was glad to have got out of the towns, where I am wont to feel unspeakably mean and disgraced,—to have left behind me for a season the bar-rooms of nothing but that savage ocean between us and Europe.

From CAPE COD

Standing on J. P. Brown's land, south side, I observed his rich and luxuriant uncut grass-lands northward, now waving under the easterly wind. It is a beautiful camilla, sweeping like waves of light and shade over the whole breadth of his land, like a low steam curling over it, imparting wonderful life to the landscape, like the light and shade of a changeable garment, . . . like waves hastening to break on a shore. It is an interesting feature, very easily overlooked, and suggests that we are wading and navigating at present in a sort of sea of grass, which yields and undulates under the wind like water; and so, perchance, the forest is seen to do from a favorable position. Early, there was that flashing light of waving pine in the horizon; now, the Camilla on grass and grain.

JOURNAL, July 4, 1860

Every day a new picture is painted and framed, held up for half an hour, in such lights as the Great Artist chooses, and then withdrawn, and the curtain falls.

And then the sun goes down, and long the afterglow gives light. And then the damask curtains glow along the western window. And now the first star is lit, and I go home.

JOURNAL, January 7, 1852

Above: Storm clouds roll over an isolated farm located on the seemingly endless plains of the Middle West. Below: A cold sun descends over a Vermont farm in the closing days of the winter months.

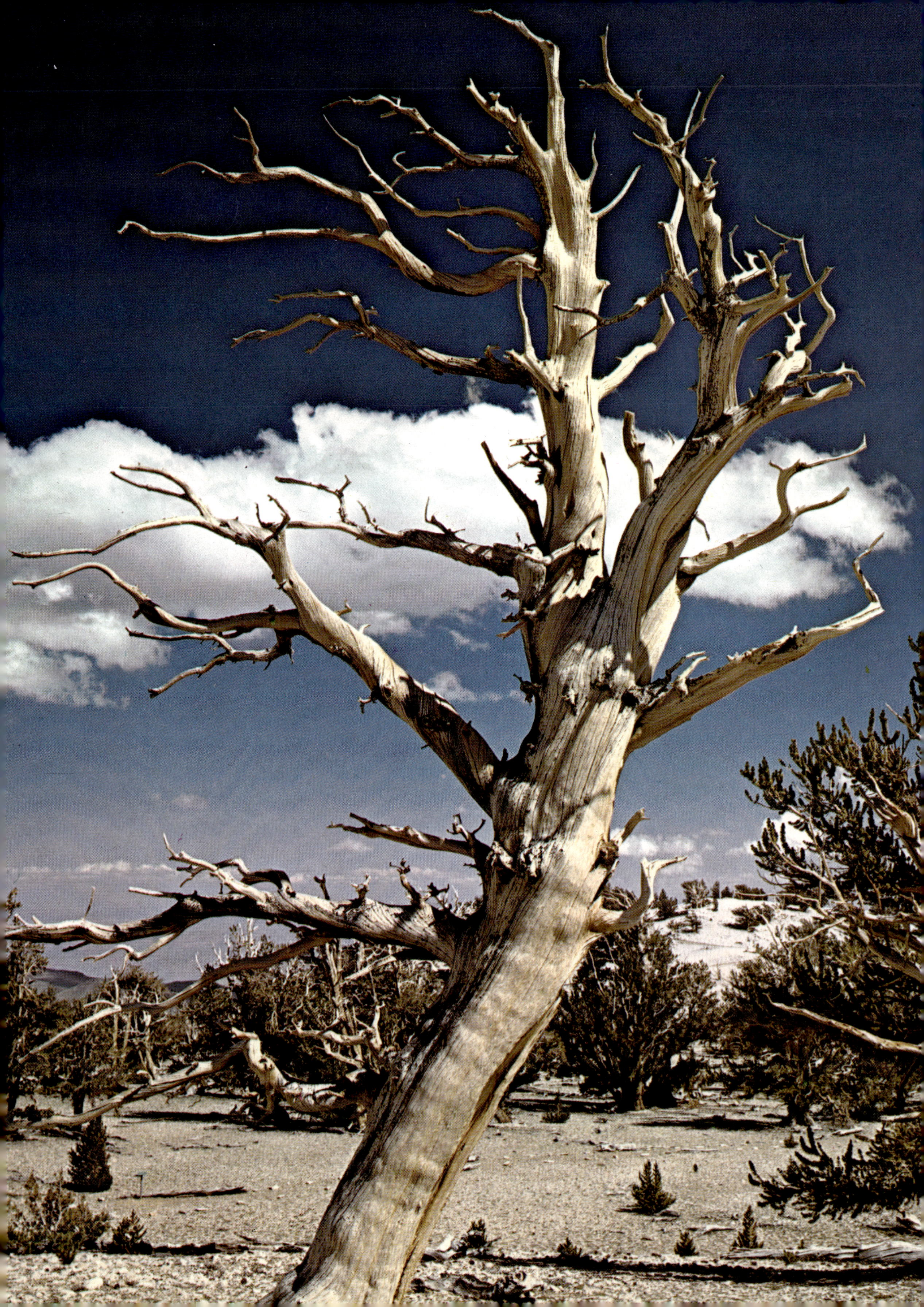

III

PHENOMENA OF NATURE

The dewy cobwebs are very thick this morning, all the earth is dripping wet...

How different the ramrod jingle of the chewink or any bird's note sounds now at 5 P.M. in the cooler, stiller air, when also the humming of insects is more distinctly heard, and perchance some impurity has begun to sink to earth strained by the air! Or is it, perchance, to be referred to the cooler, more clarified and pensive state of the mind, when dews have begun to descend in it and clarify it? Chaste eve! A certain lateness in the sound, pleasing to hear, which releases me from the obligation to return in any particular season. I have passed the Rubicon of staying out. I have said to myself, that way is not homeward; I will wander further from what I have called my home — to the home which is forever inviting me. In such an hour the freedom of the woods is offered me, and the birds sing my dispensation. In dreams the links of life are united: we forget that our friends are dead; we know them as of old.

JOURNAL, May 23, 1853

For many years I was self-appointed inspector of snow-storms and rain-storms, and did my duty faithfully.

From WALDEN

In the morning the river and adjacent country were covered with a dense fog, through which the smoke of our fire curled up like a still subtiler mist; but before we had rowed many rods, the sun arose and the fog rapidly dispersed, leaving a slight stream only to curl along the surface of the water. It was a quiet Sunday morning, with more of the auroral rosy and white than of the yellow light in it, as if it dated from earlier than the fall of man, and still preserved a heathenish integrity. . . .

From A WEEK ON THE CONCORD
AND MERRIMACK RIVERS

A spider web with clinging morning dewdrops appears as an abstract design.

There is everywhere dew on the cobwebs, little gossamer veils or scarfs as big as your hand, dropped from the fairy shoulders that danced on the grass the past night. Even where the grass was cut yesterday . . . dewy webs are as thick as anywhere, promising a fair day.

JOURNAL, July 7, 1852

A cold fog. These mornings those who walk in grass are thoroughly wetted above mid-leg. All the earth is dripping wet. I am surprised to feel how warm the water is, by contrast with the cold, foggy air. The frogs seem glad to bury themselves in it. The dewy cobwebs are very thick this morning, little napkins of the fairies spread on the grass.

JOURNAL, June 17, 1854

Low-anchored cloud, the drifting meadow, lake, sea and river...

El Capitan's granite face is hidden by a spring mist at Yosemite National Park, California.

HAZE

Woof of the sun, ethereal gauze,
Woven of Nature's richest stuffs,
Visible heat, air-water, and dry sea,
Last conquest of the eye;
Toil of the day displayed, sun-dust,
Aerial surf upon the shores of earth,
Ethereal estuary, firth of light,
Breakers of air, billows of heat,
Fine summer spray on inland seas;
Bird of the sun, transparent-winged,
Owlet of noon, soft-pinioned,
From heath or stubble rising without song;
Establish thy serenity o'er the fields.

MIST

Low-anchored cloud,
Newfoundland air,
Fountain-head and source of rivers,
Dew-cloth, dream drapery,
And napkin spread by fays;
Drifting meadow of the air,
Where bloom the daisied banks and violets,
And in whose fenny labyrinth
The bittern booms and heron wades;
Spirit of lakes and seas and rivers,
Bear only perfumes and the scent
Of healing herbs to just men's fields!

Low lying rain clouds come over the distant mountain range at Ohio Pass near Gunnison, Colorado.

... When [the] sun began to rise on this pure world, I found myself a dweller in the dazzling halls of Aurora, into which poets have had but a partial glance over the eastern hills,—drifting amid the saffron-colored clouds, and playing with the rosy fingers of the Dawn, in the very path of the Sun's chariot, and sprinkled with its dewy dust, enjoying the benignant smile, and near at hand the far-darting glances of the god. The inhabitants of earth behold commonly but the dark and shadowy under-side of heaven's pavement; it is only when seen at a favorable angle in the horizon, morning or evening, that some faint streaks of the rich lining of the clouds are revealed. But my muse would fail to convey an impression of the gorgeous tapestry by which I was surrounded, such as men see faintly reflected afar off in the chambers of the east. Here, as on earth, I saw the gracious god.

From A WEEK ON THE CONCORD AND MERRIMACK RIVERS

Water falling on rocks sounds like air falling on trees...

Going up the hill through Stow's young oak woodland, I listen to the sharp, dry rustle of the withered oak leaves. This is the voice of the wood now. It would be comparatively still and more dreary here in other respects, if it were not for these leaves that hold on. It sounds like the roar of the sea, and is enlivening and inspiriting like that, suggesting how all the land is sea-coast to the aerial ocean. It is the sound of the surf, the rut of an unseen ocean, billows of air breaking on the forest like water on itself or on sand and rocks. It rises and falls, wells and dies away, with agreeable alteration as the sea surf does. Perhaps the landsman can foretell a storm by it. It is remarkable how universal these grand murmurs are, these backgrounds of sound,—the surf, the wind in the forest, waterfalls, etc.,—which yet to the ear and in their origin are essentially one voice, the earth-voice, the breathing or snoring of the creature. The earth is our ship, and this is the sound of the wind in her rigging as we sail. Just as the inhabitant of Cape Cod hears the surf ever breaking on its shores, so we countrymen hear this kindred surf on the leaves of the forest.

JOURNAL, January 2, 1859

Again it rains, and I turn about.

The sounds of water falling on rocks and of air falling on trees are very much alike.

Though cloudy, the air excites me. Yesterday all was tight as a stricture on my breast; to-day all is loosened. It is a different element from what it was. The sides of the bushy hill where the snow is melted look, through this air, as if I were under the influence of some intoxicating liquor. The earth is not quite steady nor palpable to my senses, a little idealized. . . . The pond is covered with puddles.

JOURNAL, March 9, 1852

As I climbed the Cliffs, when I jarred the foliage, I perceived an exquisite perfume which I could not trace to its source. Ah, those fugacious universal fragrances of the meadows and woods! odors rightly mingled!

JOURNAL, June 11, 1852

In the forest the soft sounds of the waterfall are harmonized with those of the animals and the breeze in the trees.

46

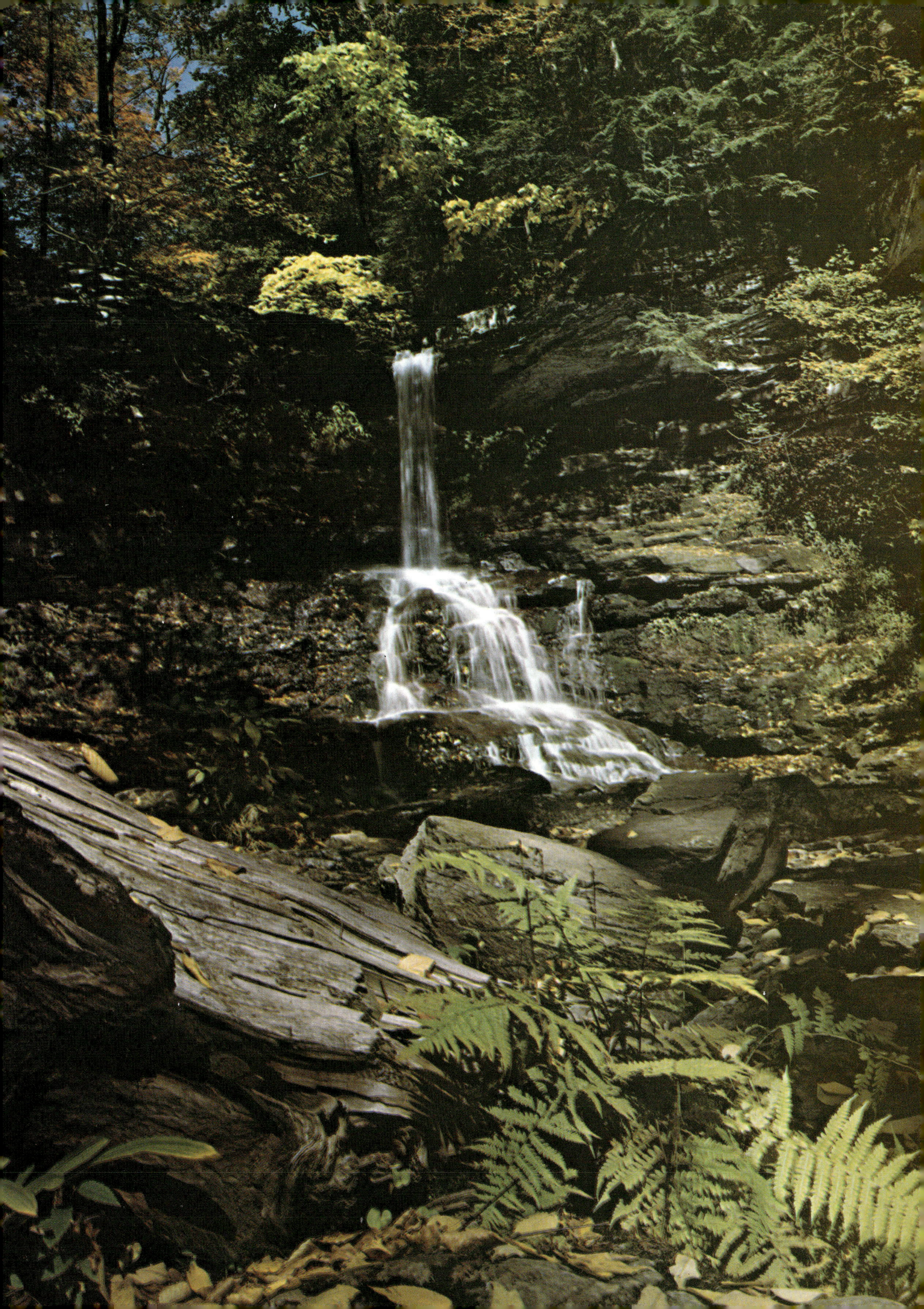

Strange that so few ever come to the woods to see how the pine lives and grows...

SMOKE

Light-winged Smoke, Icarian bird,
Melting thy pinions in thy upward flight,
Lark without song, and messenger of dawn,
Circling above the hamlets as thy nest;
Or else, departing dream, and shadowy form
Of midnight vision, gathering up thy skirts;
By night star-veiling, and by day
Darkening the light and blotting out the sun;
Go thou my incense upward from this hearth,
And ask the gods to pardon this clear flame.

The cramped and crowded city with smoke billowing from every chimney could not compare to the clean countryside, Thoreau wrote.

Strange that so few ever come to the woods to see how the pine lives and grows and spires, lifting its evergreen arms to the light,—to see its perfect success. . . .

From THE MAINE WOODS

Where my path crosses the brook in the meadow there is a singularly sweet scent in the heavy air bathing the brakes, where the brakes grow,—the fragrance of the earth, as if the dew were a distillation of the fragrant essences of Nature. . . . And now my senses are captivated again by a sweet fragrance as I enter the embowered willow causeway, and I know not if it be from a particular plant or all together,—sweet-scented vernal grass or sweet-brier. Now the sun is fairly gone, I hear the dreaming frog . . . and the cuckoo.

JOURNAL, June 14, 1851

As I sat on the high bank at the east end of Walden, . . . I saw, by a peculiar intention or dividing of the eye, a very striking subaqueous rainbow-like phenomenon. . . . Those brilliant shrubs, which were from three to a dozen feet in height, were all reflected, dimly so far as the details of leaves, etc., were concerned, but brightly as to color, and, of course, in the order in which they stood,—scarlet, yellow, green, etc.; but, there being a slight ripple on the surface, these reflections were not true to their height though true to their breadth, but were extended downward with mathematical perpendicularity, three or four times too far, forming sharp pyramids of the several colors, gradually reduced to mere dusky points. The effect of this prolongation of the reflection was a very pleasing softening and blending of the colors, especially when a small bush of one bright tint stood directly before another of a contrary and equally bright tint. It was just as if you were to brush firmly aside with your hand or a brush a fresh line of paint of various colors, or so many lumps of friable colored powders.

JOURNAL, October 7, 1857

The pine tree has a spicy, yet sweet-scented odor which mixes well with other smells in the forest.

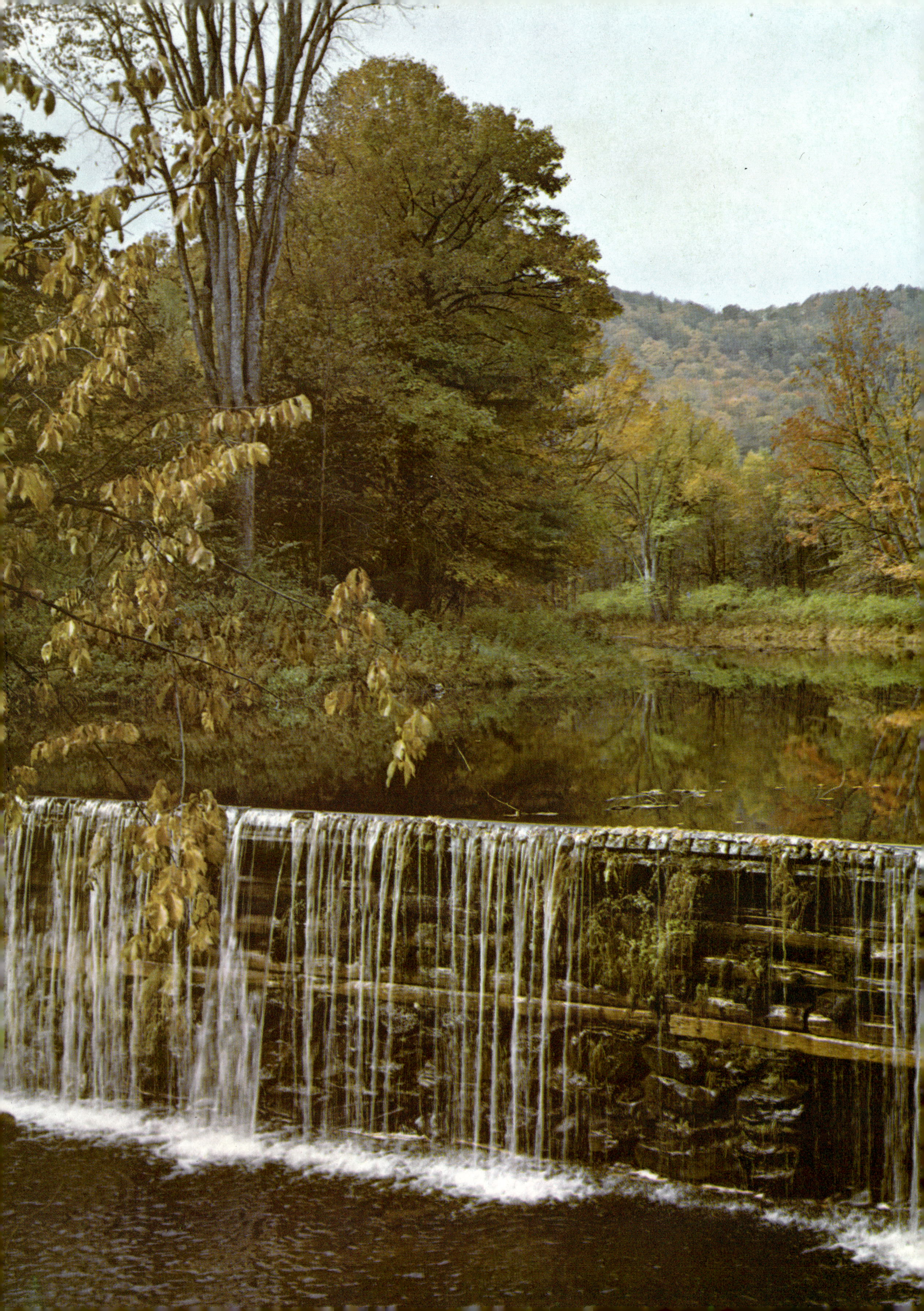

IV
FOCUSING DOWN ON NATURE

The lowly fungus is radiant to a poet's eye...

It is remarkable how little any but a lichenist will observe on the bark of trees. The mass of men have but the vaguest and most indefinite notion of mosses, as a sort of shreds and fringes, and the world in which the lichenist dwells is much further from theirs than one side of this earth from the other. They see bark as if they saw it not. . . .

Each phase of nature, while not invisible, is yet not too distinct and obtrusive. It is there to be found when we look for it, but not demanding our attention. It is like a silent but sympathizing companion in whose company we retain most of the advantages of solitude, with whom we can walk and talk, or be silent, naturally, without the necessity of talking in a strain foreign to the place.

I know of but one or two persons with whom I can afford to walk. With most the walk degenerates into a more vigorous use of your legs, ludicrously purposeless, while you are discussing some mighty argument, each one having his say, spoiling each other's day, worrying one another with conversation, hustling one another with our conversation. I know of no use in the walking part in this case, except that we may seem to be getting on together towards some goal; but of course we keep our original distance all the way. Jumping every wall and ditch with vigor in the vain hope of shaking your companion off. Trying to kill two birds with one stone, though they sit at opposite points of compass, to see nature and do the honors to one who does not.

JOURNAL, November 8, 1858

Nature doth thus kindly heal every wound. By the mediation of a thousand little mosses and fungi, the most unsightly objects become radiant of beauty. There seem to be two sides of this world, presented us at different times, as we see things in growth or dissolution, in life or death. For seen with the eye of the poet, as God sees them, all things are alive and beautiful; but seen with the historical eye, or eye of the memory, they are dead and offensive. If we see Nature as pausing, immediately all mortifies and decays; but seen as progressing, she is beautiful.

JOURNAL, March 13, 1842

The simplest and most lumpish fungus has a peculiar interest to us, compared with a mere mass of earth, because it is so obviously organic and related to ourselves, however remote. It is the expression of an idea; growth according to a law; matter not dormant, not raw, but inspired, appropriated by spirit. If I take up a handful of earth, however separately interesting the particles may be, their relation to one another appears to be that of mere juxtaposition generally. I might have thrown them together thus. But the humblest fungus betrays a life akin to our own. It is a successful poem in its kind. There is suggested something superior to any particle of matter, in the idea or mind which uses and arranges the particles.

JOURNAL, October 10, 1858

In this fresh evening each blade and leaf looks as if it had been dipped in an icy liquid greenness. Let eyes that ache come here and look. . . .

JOURNAL, June 30, 1840

The fungi, by breaking down organic matter to simpler forms, maintain nature's progress.

We sit by the side of little Goose Pond . . . to watch the ripples on it. Now it is merely smooth, and then there drops down on to it, deep as it lies amid the hills, a sharp and narrow blast of the icy north wind careening above, striking it, perhaps, by a point or an edge, and swiftly spreading along it, making a dark-blue ripple. Now four or five windy bolts, sharp or blunt, strike it at once and spread different ways. The boisterous but playful north wind evidently stoops from a considerable height to dally with this fair pool which it discerns beneath. You could sit there and watch these blue shadows playing over the surface like the light and shade on changeable silk, for hours. It reminds me, too, of the swift Camilla on a field [of] grain. The wind often touches the water only by the finest points or edges. It is thus when you look in some measure from the sun, but if you move around so as to come more opposite to him, then these dark-blue ripples are all sparkles too bright to look at, for now you see the sides of the wavelets which reflect the sun to you.

JOURNAL, April 9, 1859

The splendid rhodora now sets the swamps on fire with its masses of rich color. It is one of the first flowers to catch the eye at a distance in masses,—so naked, unconcealed by its own leaves.

JOURNAL, May 17, 1854

Found two lilies open in the very shallow inlet of the meadow. Exquisitely beautiful, and unlike anything else that we have, is the first white lily just expanded in some shallow lagoon where the water is leaving it,—perfectly fresh and pure, before the insects have discovered it. How admirable its purity! How innocently sweet its fragrance! How significant that the rich, black mud of our dead stream produces the water-lily,— out of that fertile slime springs this spotless purity! It is remarkable that those flowers which are most emblematical of purity should grow in the mud.

JOURNAL, June 20, 1853

These aquatic plants dwell in bogs,
marshes and the edges of slow-flowing streams.

Some ponds are thought to be bottomless...

While men believe in the infinite, some ponds will be thought to be bottomless.

From WALDEN

Sitting on the Conantum house sill (still left), I see two and perhaps three young striped squirrels, two-thirds grown, within fifteen or twenty feet, one or more on the wall and another on the ground. Their tails are rather imperfect, as their bodies. They are running about, yet rather feebly, nibbling the grass, etc., or sitting upright, looking very cunning. The broad white line above and below the eye make it look very long as well as large, and the black and white stripe on its sides, curved as it sits, are very conspicuous and pretty. Who striped the squirrel's side? Several times I saw two approach each other and playfully and, as it were, affectionately put their paws and noses to each other's faces. Yet this was done very deliberately and affectionately. There was no rudeness nor excessive activity in the sport. At length the old one appears, larger and much more bluish, and shy, and, with a sharp cluck or chip, calls the others gradually to her and draws them off along the wall, they from time to time frisking ahead of her, then she ahead of them. The hawks must get many of these inexperienced creatures.

JOURNAL, June 25, 1858

One of the most common wild flowers, the painted trillium, is found in northern woodlands and alongside brooks.

I saw a delicate flower had grown up two feet high
Between the horses' feet and the wheel track,
Which Dakin's and Maynard's wagons had
Passed over many a time.
An inch more to right or left had sealed its fate,
Or an inch higher. Yet it lived to flourish
As much as if it had a thousand acres
Of untrodden space around it and never
Knew the danger it incurred.
It did not borrow trouble nor invite an
Evil fate by apprehending it.

JOURNAL, September 1850

A great part of the pine-needles have just fallen. See the carpet of pale-brown needles under this pine. How light it lies upon the grass, and that great rock, and the wall, resting thick on its top and its shelves, and on the bushes and underwood, hanging lightly! They are not yet flat and reddish, but a more delicate pale brown, and lie up light as joggle-sticks, just dropped. The ground is nearly concealed by them. How beautifully they die, making cheerfully their annual contribution to the soil! They fall to rise again; as if they knew that it was not one annual deposit alone that made this rich mold in which pine trees grow. They live in the soil whose fertility and bulk they increase, and in the forests that spring from it.

JOURNAL, October 16, 1857

I well remember the time this year when I first heard the dream of the toads. I was laying out house-lots on Little River in Haverhill. We had had some raw, cold and wet weather. But this day was remarkably warm and pleasant, and I had thrown off my outside coat. I was going home to dinner, past a shallow pool, which was green with springing grass, . . . when it occurred to me that I heard the dream of the toad. It rang through and filled all the air, though I had not heard it once. And I turned my companion's attention to it, but he did not appear to perceive it as a new sound in the air. Loud and prevailing as it is, most men do not notice it at all. It is to them, perchance, a sort of simmering or seething of all nature. That afternoon the dream of the toads rang through the elms by Little River and affected the thoughts of men, though they were not conscious that they heard it.

How watchful we must be to keep the crystal well that we are made, clear! — that it be not made turbid by our contact with the world. . . .

JOURNAL, October 26, 1853

This is the aspect under which the Musketaquid might be represented at this season: a long, smooth lake, reflecting the bare willows and button beeches, the stubble, and the wool-grass on its tussock, a muskrat-cabin or two conspicuously on its margin amid the unsightly tops of pontederia, and a bittern disappearing on undulating wing around a bend.

JOURNAL, November 1, 1855

It occurred to me I had heard the dream of the toad that most men do not notice...

As the day closes the toads and frogs begin to croak from their homes near ponds and rivers.

Evergreens and pines add a natural color to the gray Valley of the Ten Peaks on Moraine Lake near Banff, Alberta, Can.

This afternoon, being on Fair Haven Hill, I heard the sound of a saw, and soon after from the Cliff saw two men sawing down a noble pine beneath, about forty rods off. I resolved to watch it till it fell, the last of a dozen or more which were left when the forest was cut and for fifteen years have waved in solitary majesty over the sprout-land. I saw them like beavers or insects gnawing at the trunk of this noble tree, the diminutive manikins with their cross-cut saw which could scarcely span it. . . . I watch closely to see when it begins to move. Now the sawers stop, and with an axe open it a little on the side towards which it leans, that it may break the faster, and now their saw goes again. Now surely it is going; it is inclined one quarter of the quadrant, and, breathless, I expect its crashing fall. But no, I was mistaken; it has not moved an inch; it stands at the same angle as at first. It is fifteen minutes yet to its fall. Still its branches wave in the wind, as if it were destined to stand for a century, and the wind soughs through its needles as of yore; it is still a forest tree, the most majestic tree that waves over Musketaquid. The silvery sheen of sunlight is reflected from its needles; it still affords an inaccessible crotch for the squirrel's nest; not a lichen has forsaken its mast-like stem, its raking mast,— the hill is the hulk. Now, now's the moment! The manikins at its base are fleeing from their crime. They have dropped the guilty saw and axe. How slowly and majestically it starts! As if it were only swayed by a summer breeze, and would return without a sigh to its location in the air.

And now it fans the hillside with its fall, and lies down to its bed in the valley, from which it is never to rise, as softly as a feather, folding its green mantle about it like a warrior, as if, tired of standing, it embraces the earth with silent joy, returning its elements to the dust again. But, hark! . . . You only saw, but did not hear. There now comes up a deafening crash to these rocks, advertising [to] you that even trees do not die without a groan. . . .

It is lumber. . . . When the fish hawk in the spring revisits the banks of the Musketaquid, he will circle in vain to find his accustomed perch, and the hen-hawk will mourn for the pines lofty enough to protect his brood. . . . I hear no knell tolled, I see no procession of mourners in the streets, or the woodland aisles. The squirrel has leaped to another tree; the hawk has circled farther off, and has now settled upon a new eyrie, but the woodman is preparing [to] lay his axe to the root of that also.

JOURNAL, December 30, 1851

Shade is produced and the birds are concealed...

When I am opposite the end of the willow-row, seeing the osiers of perhaps two years old all in a mess, they are seen to be very distinctly yellowish beneath and scarlet above. They are fifty rods off. Here is the same chemistry that colors the leaf or fruit, coloring the bark. It is generally, perhaps always, the upper part of the twig, the more recent growth, that is the higher-colored and more flower or fruit like. So leaves are more ethereal the higher up and farther from the root. In the bark of the twigs, indeed, is the more permanent flower or fruit. The flower falls in spring or summer, the fruit and leaves fall or wither in autumn, but the blushing twigs retain their color throughout the winter and appear more brilliant than ever the succeeding spring. They are winter fruit. It adds greatly to the pleasure of late November . . . to look into these mazes of twigs. . . .

JOURNAL, March 17, 1859

I noticed yesterday the first conspicuous silvery sheen from the needles of the white pine waving in the wind. A small one was conspicuous by the side of the road more than a quarter mile ahead. I suspect that those plumes which have been oppressed or contracted by snow and ice are not only dried but opened and spread by the wind.

JOURNAL, February 25, 1860

Within a little more than a fortnight the woods, from bare twigs, have become a sea of verdure, and young shoots have contended with one another in the race. The leaves are unfurled all over the country. . . . Shade is produced, and the birds are concealed and their economies go forward uninterruptedly, and a covert is afforded to animals generally. But thousands of worms and insects are preying on the leaves while they are young and tender. Myriads of little parasols are suddenly spread all the country over, to shield the earth and the roots of the trees from the parching heat, and they begin to flutter and rustle in the breeze. Checkerberry shoots . . . are now just fit to eat. . . .

JOURNAL, June 1, 1854

Above: Ice forms interesting patterns on a tree in the Catskills. Below: The site of Thoreau's cabin near Walden Pond.

*My temple
is the swamp
and the birches...*

When the playful breeze drops in the pool, it springs to right and left, quick as a kitten playing with dead leaves, clapping her paw on them. Sometimes it merely raises a single wave at one point, as if a fish darted near the surface.

JOURNAL, April 9, 1859

A little sunshine at rising. I, standing by the river, see it first reflected from E. Wood's windows before I can see the sun. Standing there, I hear that same stertorous note of a frog or two as was heard the 13th, apparently from quite across all this flood, and which I have so often observed before. What kind is it?

JOURNAL, April 15, 1856

In the twilight I went through the swamp, and the yellow birches sent forth a dull-yellow gleam which each time made my heart beat faster. Occasionally you come to a dead and leaning white birch, beset with large fungi like ears or little shelves, with a rounded edge above. I walked with the yellow birch. The prinos is green within. If there were Druids whose temples were the oak groves, my temple is the swamp. Sometimes I was in doubt about a birch whose vest was buttoned smooth and dark, till I came nearer and saw the yellow gleaming through, or where a button was off.

JOURNAL, January 4, 1853

The water willow, *salix Purshiana,* when it is of large size and entire, is the most graceful and ethereal of our trees. Its masses of light green foliage, piled one upon another to the height of twenty or thirty feet, seemed to float on the surface of the water, while the slight gray stems and the shore were hardly visible between them. No tree is so wedded to the water, and harmonizes so well with still streams. It is even more graceful than the weeping willow, or any pendulous trees, which dip their branches in the stream instead of being buoyed up by it. Its limbs curved outward over the surface as if attracted by it. It had not a New England but an oriental character, reminding us of trim Persian gardens of Haroun Alraschid, and the artificial lakes of the east.

From A WEEK ON THE CONCORD
AND MERRIMACK RIVERS

Heavier foliage on the water side and poor soil support for the roots force the river birch to lean toward the water.

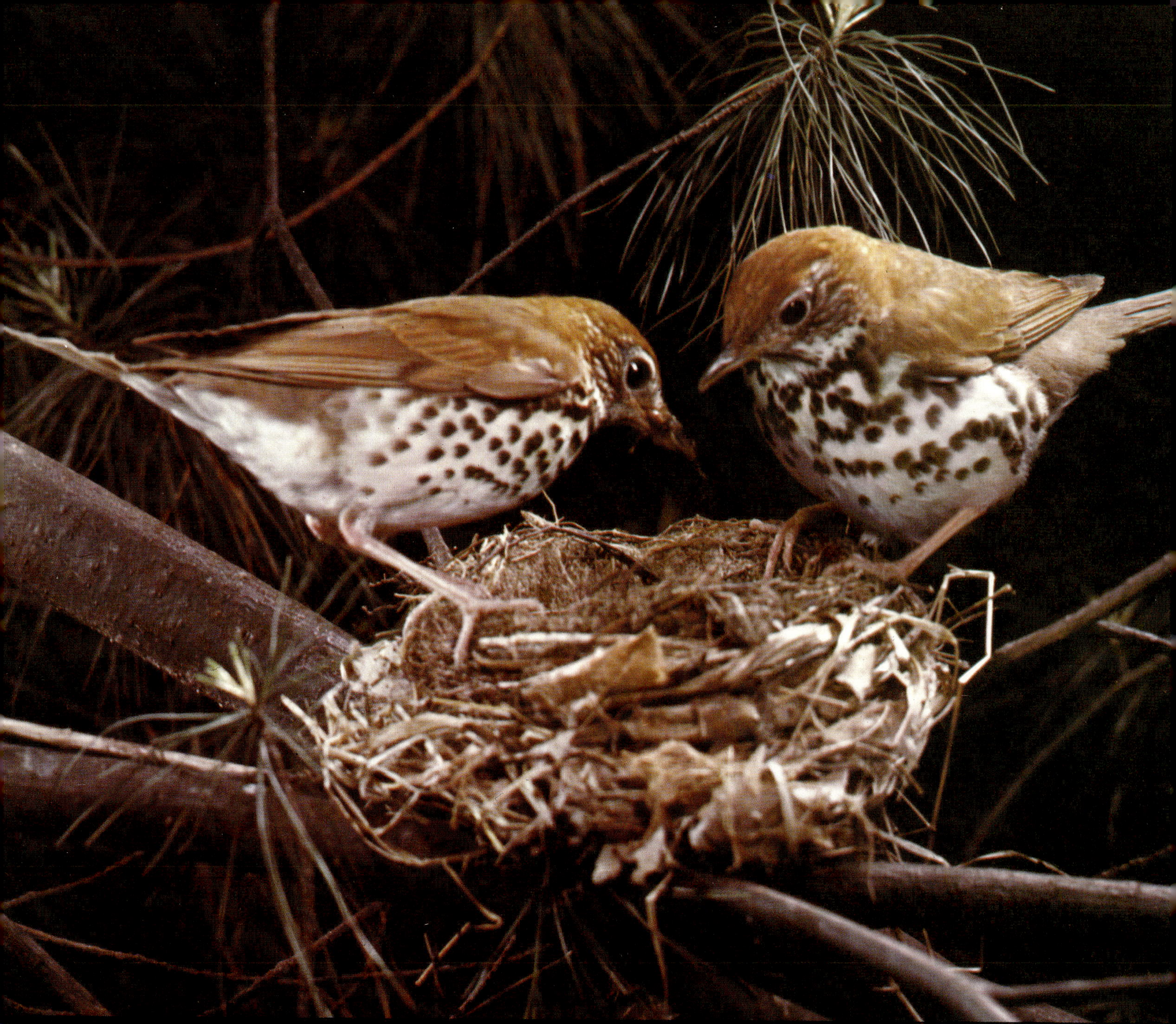

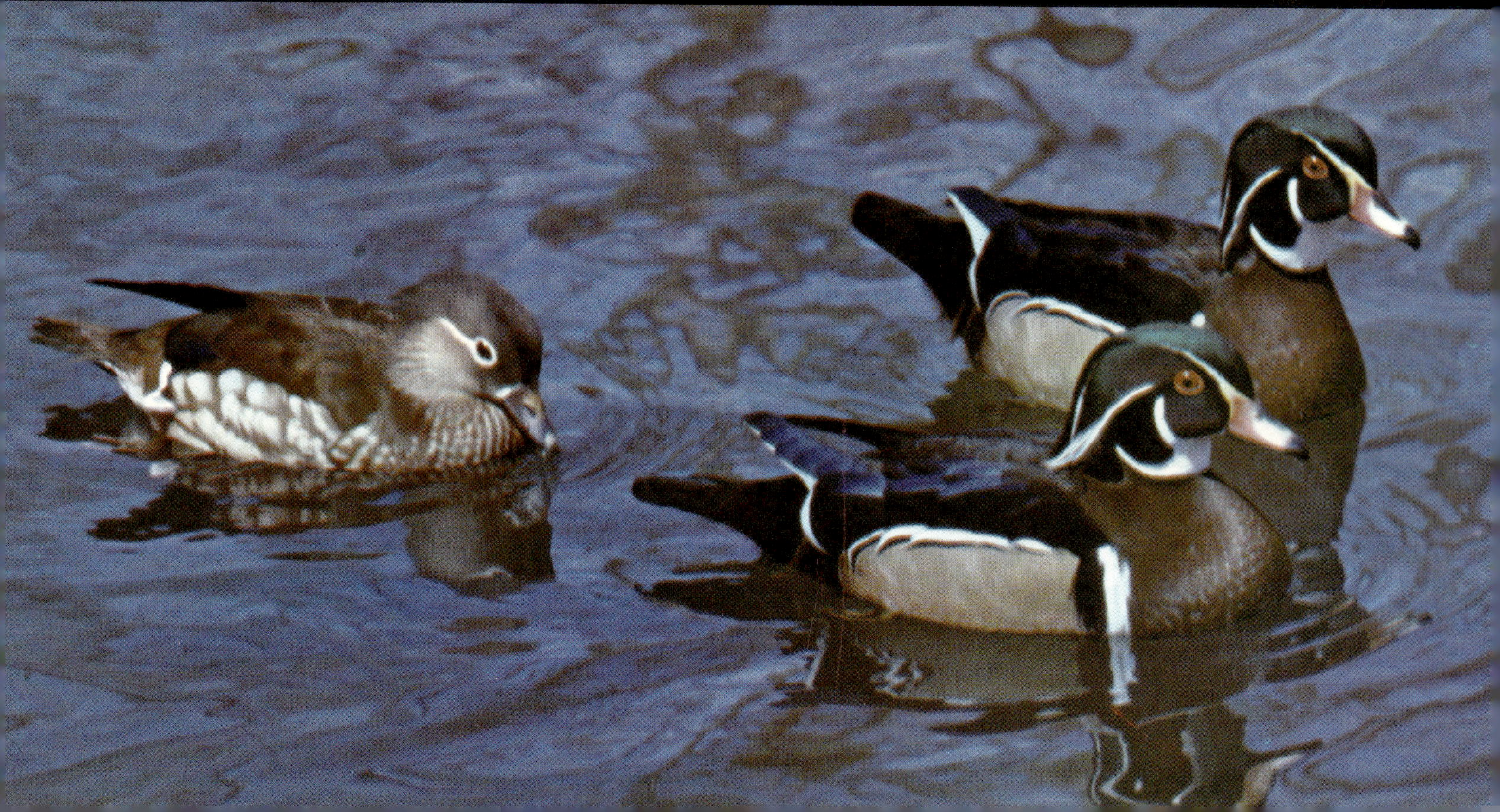

Left: Bluebird. Far left: Wood Thrush. Below: Wood Ducks.

V
A NEST
OF BIRDS

63

Thoreau enjoyed long sojourns in the woods and liked his shelter to be close to nature.

As I come over the hill, I hear the wood thrush singing his evening lay. This is the only bird whose note affects me like music, affects the flow and tenor of my thoughts, my fancy and imagination. It lifts and exhilarates me. It is inspiring. It is a medicative draught to my soul. It is an elixir to my eyes and a fountain of youth to all my senses. It changes all hours to an eternal morning. It banishes all trivialness. It reinstates me in my dominion, makes me the lord of creation, is chief musician of my court. This minstrel sings in a time, a heroic age, with which no event in the village can be contemporary. How can they be contemporary when only the latter is *temporary* at all? . . . So there is something in the music of the cow-bell, something sweeter and more nutritious, than in the milk which the farmers drink. This thrush's song is a *ranz des vaches* to me. I long for wildness, a nature which I cannot put my foot through, woods where the wood thrush forever sings, where the hours are early morning ones, and there is dew on the grass, and the day is forever unproved, where I might have a fertile unknown for a soil about me. I would go after the cows, I would watch the flocks of Admetus there forever, only for my board and clothes, a New Hampshire everlasting and unfallen. . . . All that was ripest and fairest in the wildness and the wild man is preserved and transmitted to us in the strain of the wood thrush. It is the mediator between barbarism and civilization. It is unrepentant as Greece.

JOURNAL, June 22, 1853

At Corner Spring, stood listening to a catbird, sounding a good way off. Was surprised to detect the singer within a rod and a half on a low twig, the ventriloquist. Should not have believed it was he, if I had not seen the movements of his throat, corresponding to each note,—looking at this near singer whose notes sounded so far away.

JOURNAL, May 13, 1853

A catbird has her nest in our grove. We cast out strips of white cotton cloth all of which she picked up and used. I saw a bird flying across the street with so long a strip of cloth, or the like, the other day, and so slowly that at first I thought it was a little boy's kite with a long tail. The catbird sings less now, while its mate is sitting, or maybe taking care of her young, and probably this is the case with robins and birds generally.

JOURNAL, June 2, 1860

The friendly, inquisitive catbird lives in thickets and hedgerows. This songbird never repeats a phrase.

He was indeed a silly loon — again he laughed long and loud with more reason than before...

As I was paddling along the north shore one very calm October afternoon—for such days especially they settle on to the lakes, like the milkweed down—having looked in vain over the pond for a loon, suddenly one sailing out from the shore toward the middle a few rods in front of me set up his wild laugh and betrayed himself. I pursued with a paddle and he dived, but when he came up I was nearer than before. He dived again, but I miscalculated the direction he would take, and we were fifty rods apart when he came to the surface this time, for I had helped to widen the interval; and again he laughed long and loud, and with more reason than before. He maneuvered so cunningly that I could not get within half-a-dozen rods of him.

Inept on land, facile in water, the loon builds his nest on the shoreline so he can escape in case of danger.

Each time, when he came to the surface, turning his head this way and that, he coolly surveyed the water and the land, and apparently chose his course so that he might come up where there was the widest expanse of water and at the greatest distance from the boat. It was surprising how quickly he made up his mind and put his resolve into execution. He led me at once to the widest part of the pond, and could not be driven from it. While he was thinking one thing in his brain, I was endeavoring to divine his thought in mine. It was a pretty game, played on the smooth surface of the pond, a man against a loon. Suddenly your adversary's checker disappears beneath the board, and the problem is to place yours nearest to where he will appear again. Sometimes he would come up unexpectedly on the opposite side of me, having apparently passed directly under the boat. So long-winded was he and so unwearible, that when he had swum farthest he would immediately plunge again, nevertheless; and then no wit could divine where in the deep pond, beneath the smooth surface, he might be speeding his way like a fish, for he had time and ability to visit the bottom of the pond in its deepest part. It is said that loons have been caught in the New York lakes eighty feet beneath the surface, with hooks set for trout — though Walden is deeper than that. How surprised must the fishes be to see this ungainly visitor from another sphere speeding his way amid their schools! Yet he appeared to know his course as surely under water as on the surface, and swam much faster there. Once or twice I saw a ripple where he approached the surface, just put his head out to reconnoiter, and instantly dived again. I found that it was as well for me to rest on my oars and wait his reappearing, as to endeavor to calculate where he would rise; for again and again, when I was straining my eyes over the surface one way, I would suddenly be startled by his unearthly laugh behind me. But why, after displaying so much cunning, did he invariably betray himself the moment he came up, by that loud laugh? Did not his white breast enough betray him? He was indeed a silly loon, I thought. I could commonly hear the splash of the water when he came up, and so also detect him. But after an hour he seemed as fresh as ever, dived as willingly, and swam yet farther than at first. It was surprising to see how serenely he sailed off with unruffled breast when he came to the surface, doing all the work with his webbed feet beneath.

From WALDEN

*It was a summer eve
the air did gently heave...*

TO THE MAIDEN IN THE EAST

Low in the eastern sky
Is set thy glancing eye;
And though its gracious light
Ne'er riseth to my sight,
Yet every star that climbs
Above the gnarled limbs
    Of yonder hill,
Conveys thy gentle will.

Believe I knew thy thought,
And that the zephyrs brought
Thy kindest wishes through,
As mine they bear to you,
That some attentive cloud
Did pause amid the crowd
    Over my head,
While gentle things were said.

Believe the thrushes sung,
And that the flower-bells rung,
That herbs exhaled their scent,
And beasts knew what was meant,
The trees a welcome waved,
And lakes their margins laved,
    When thy free mind
To my retreat did wind.

It was a summer eve,
The air did gently heave
While yet a low-hung cloud
Thy eastern skies did shroud;
The lightning's silent gleam,
Startling my drowsy dream,
    Seemed like the flash
Under thy dark eyelash.

Still will I strive to be
As if thou wert with me;
Whatever path I take,
It shall be for thy sake,
Of gentle slope and wide,
As thou wert by my side,
    Without a root
To trip thy gentle foot.

I'll walk with gentle pace,
And choose the smoothest place,
And careful dip the oar,
And shun the winding shore,
And gently steer my boat
Where water-lilies float,
    And cardinal flowers
Stand in their sylvan bowers.

At the end of a summer's day, a quiet, thoughtful peace comes over a lake.

Sunlight catches a young gull in motionless flight. Light body weight allows him to fly long distances.

Every landscape which is dreary enough has a certain beauty to my eyes, and in this instance its permanent qualities were enhanced by the weather. Everything told of the sea, even when we did not see its waste or hear its roar. For birds there were gulls, and for carts in the fields, boats turned bottom upward against the houses, and sometimes the rib of a whale was woven into the fence by the road-side. The trees were, if possible, rarer than the houses. . . .

From CAPE COD

At Ball's Hill see five summer ducks, a brood now grown, feeding amid the pads on the opposite side of the river, with a whitish ring, perhaps nearly around neck. A rather shrill squeaking quack when they go off. It is remarkable how much more game you will see if you are in the habit of *sitting* in the fields and woods. As you pass along with a noise it hides itself, but presently comes forth again.

JOURNAL, August 6, 1855

The birds carry the skies on their backs...

As we thus dipped our way along between fresh masses of foliage overrun with the grape and smaller flowering vines, the surface was so calm, and both air and water so transparent, that the flight of a kingfisher or robin over the river was as distinctly seen reflected in the water below as in the air above. The birds seemed to flit through submerged groves, alighting on the yielding sprays, and their clear notes to come up from below. We were uncertain whether the water floated the land, or the land held the water in its bosom. . . . For every oak and birch too growing on the hilltop, as well as for these elms and willows, we knew that there was a graceful, ethereal and ideal tree making down from the roots, and sometimes Nature in high tides brings her mirror to its foot and makes it visible. The stillness was intense and almost conscious, as if it were a natural Sabbath. The air was so elastic and crystalline that it had the same effect on the landscape that a glass has on a picture, to give it an ideal remoteness and perfection. The landscape was clothed in a mild and quiet light, in which the woods and fences checkered and partitioned it with new regularity, and rough and uneven fields stretched away with lawn-like smoothness to the horizon, and the clouds, finely distinct and picturesque, seemed a fit drapery to hang over fairy-land. The world seemed decked for some holyday or prouder pageantry, with silken streamers flying, and the course of our lives to wind on before us like a green lane into a country maze, at the season when fruit trees are in blossom.

Why should not our whole life and its scenery be actually thus fair and distinct? All our lives want a suitable background. . . . Character always secures for itself this advantage, and is thus distinct and unrelated to near or trivial objects whether things or persons.

From A WEEK ON THE CONCORD
AND MERRIMACK RIVERS

The blue-bird carries the sky on his back.

JOURNAL, April 3, 1852

The still air and soft light on trees made apparent to Thoreau man's need for a befitting environment.

How well suited the lining of a bird's nest, not only for the comfort of the young, but to keep the eggs from breaking! Fine elastic grass stems or root fibers, pine needles, or hair, or the like. These tender and brittle things which you can hardly carry in cotton lie there without harm.

JOURNAL, June 6, 1856

In my boating of late I have several times scared up a couple of summer ducks of this year, bred in our meadows. They allowed me to come quite near, and helped to people the river. I have not seen them for some days. Would you know the end of our intercourse? Goodwin shot them, and Mrs. ——, who never sailed on the river, ate them. Of course, she knows not what she did. What if I should eat her canary? Thus we share each other's sins as well as burdens. The lady who watches admiringly the matador shares his deed. They belonged to me, as much as to any one, when they were alive, but it is considered of more importance that Mrs. —— should taste the flavor of them dead than that I should enjoy the beauty of them alive.

JOURNAL, August 16, 1858

Mr. Farmer tells me that one Sunday he went to his barn, having nothing to do, and thought he would watch the swallows, republican swallows. The old bird was feeding her young, and he sat within fifteen feet, overlooking them. There were five young, and he was curious to know how each received its share; and as often as the bird came with a fly, the one at the door (or opening) took it, and then they all hitched round one notch, so that a new one was presented at the door, who received the next fly; and this was the invariable order, the same one never received two flies in succession. At last the old bird brought a very small fly, and the young one that swallowed it did not desert his ground but waited to receive the next, but when the bird came with another, of the usual size, she commenced a loud and long scolding at the little one, till it resigned its place, and the next in succession received the fly.

JOURNAL, November 9, 1857

VI
OF TIME AND MAN

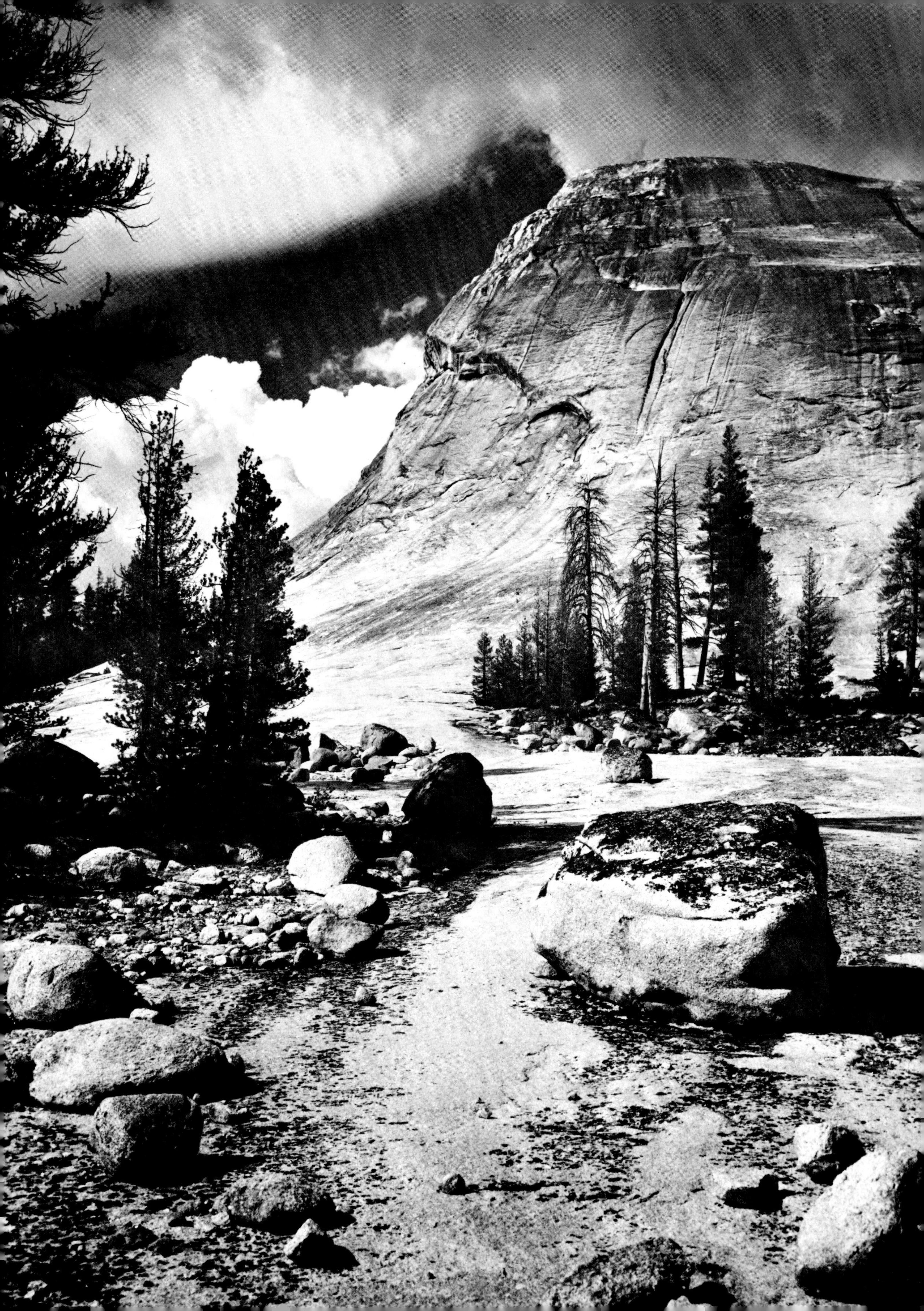

Time will make most materials harmonize...

Each new year is a surprise to us. We find that we had virtually forgotten the note of each bird, and when we hear it again it is remembered like a dream, reminding us of a previous state of existence. How happens it that the associations it awakens are always pleasing, never saddening; reminiscences of our sanest hours? The voice of nature is always encouraging.

JOURNAL, March 18, 1858

It seems natural that rocks which have lain under the heavens so long should be gray, as it were an intermediate color between the heavens and the earth. The air is the thin paint in which they have been dipped and brushed with the wind. Water, which is more fluid and like the sky in its nature, is still more like it in color. Time will make the most discordant materials harmonize.

JOURNAL, June 23, 1852

As if you could kill time without injuring eternity.

From WALDEN

The mass of men lead lives of quiet desperation. What is called resignation is confirmed desperation. From the desperate city you go into the desperate country, and have to console yourself with the bravery of minks and muskrats. A stereotyped but unconscious despair is concealed even under what are called the games and amusements of mankind. There is no play in them, for this comes after work. But it is a characteristic of wisdom not to do desperate things.

From WALDEN

Ice-polished Lambert Dome at Yosemite National Park reveals the effects of the last glacier.

Freer air brings forth more fruits and flowers...

SIC VITA

I am a parcel of vain strivings tied
    By a chance bond together,
  Dangling this way and that, their links
    Were made so loose and wide,
      Methinks,
      For milder weather.

A bunch of violets without their roots,
    And sorrel intermixed,
  Encircled by a wisp of straw
    Once coiled about their shoots,
      The law
      By which I'm fixed.

A popular garden flower, the columbine, was named from the Latin word for dove.

A nosegay which Time clutched from out
    Those fair Elysian fields,
  With weeds and broken stems, in haste,
    Doth make the rabble rout
      That waste
      The day he yields.

And here I bloom for a short hour unseen,
    Drinking my juices up,
  With no root in the land
    To keep my branches green,
      But stand
      In a bare cup.

Some tender buds were left upon my stem
    In mimicry of life,
  But ah! the children will not know,
    Till time has withered them,
      The woe
      With which they're rife.

But now I see I was not plucked for naught,
    And after in life's vase
  Of glass set while I might survive,
    But by a kind hand brought
      Alive
      To a strange place.

That stock thus thinned will soon redeem its hours,
    And by another year,
  Such as God knows, with freer air,
    More fruits and fairer flowers
      Will bear,
      While I droop here.

A deer is silhouetted against the cloud-filled valley below the ridge on which he grazes in the Olympic Mountains.

MEN SAY THEY KNOW MANY THINGS

Men say they know many things;
But lo! they have taken wings,—
The arts and sciences,
And a thousand appliances;
The wind that blows
Is all that any body knows.

I never found the companion that was so companionable as solitude...

Most of the luxuries, and many of the so-called comforts, of life are not only not indispensable, but positive hindrances to the elevation of mankind.

From WALDEN

If a man does not keep pace with his companions, perhaps it is because he hears a different drummer. Let him step to the music which he hears, however measured or far away.

From WALDEN

Through our own recovered innocence we discern the innocence of our neighbors.

From WALDEN

There are from time to time mornings, both in summer and in winter, when especially the world seems to begin anew, beyond which memory need not go, for not behind them is yesterday and our past life; when, as in the morning of a hoar frost, there are visible the effects as of a certain creative energy, the world has visibly been recreated in the night. Mornings of creation, I call them. In the midst of these marks of a creative energy recently active, while the sun is rising with more than usual splendor, I look back . . . for the era of this creation, not into the night, but to a dawn for which no man ever rose early enough. A morning which carries us back beyond the Mosaic creation, where crystallizations are fresh and unmelted. It is the poet's hour. Mornings when men are new-born, men who have the seeds of life in them.

JOURNAL, January 26, 1853

I never found the companion that was so companionable as solitude. We are for the most part more lonely when we go abroad among men than when we stay in our chambers. A man thinking or working is always alone, let him be where he will.

From WALDEN

Our life is frittered away by detail.... Simplify, simplify.

From WALDEN

A heavy snow wraps the trees in strange shapes near Mt. Scott at Crater Lake National Park, Oregon.

The ice and snow of the frozen marsh will thwart the perennial cattail in its attempt to seed itself.

I went to the woods because I wished to live deliberately, to front only the essential facts of life, and see if I could not learn what it had to teach, and not, when I came to die, discover that I had not lived.

From WALDEN

To him whose elastic and vigorous thought keeps pace with the sun, the day is a perpetual morning.

From WALDEN

There are a thousand hacking at the branches of evil to one who is striking at the root.

From WALDEN

Beware of all enterprises that require new clothes.

From WALDEN

There is no odor so bad as that which arises from goodness tainted.

From WALDEN

The man who goes alone can start today; but he who travels with another must wait till that other is ready.

From WALDEN

A pine cut down, a dead pine, is no more a pine than a dead human carcass is a man. . . . Every creature is better alive than dead, men and moose and pine-trees, and he who understands it aright will rather preserve its life than destroy it.

From THE MAINE WOODS

The poet's, commonly, is not a logger's path, but a woodman's. The logger and pioneer have preceded him, like John the Baptist; eaten the wild honey, it may be, but the locusts also; banished decaying wood and the spongy mosses which feed on it, and built hearths and humanized Nature for him.

But there are spirits of a yet more liberal culture, to whom no simplicity is barren. There are not only stately pines, but fragile flowers, like the orchises, commonly described as too delicate for cultivation, which derive their nutriment from the crudest mass of peat. These remind us, that, not only for strength, but for beauty, the poet must, from time to time, travel the logger's path and the Indian's trail, to drink at some new and more bracing fountain of the Muses, far in the recesses of the wilderness.

The kings of England formerly had their forests "to hold the king's game," for sport or food, sometimes destroying villages to create or extend them; and I think that they were impelled by a true instinct. Why should not we, who have renounced the king's authority, have our national preserves, where no villages need be destroyed, in which the bear and panther, and some even of the hunter race, may still exist, and not be "civilized off the face of the earth,"—our forests, not to hold the king's game merely, but to hold and preserve the king himself also, the lord of creation,—not for idle sport or food, but for inspiration and our own true recreation? or shall we, like villains, grub them all up, poaching on our own national domains?

From THE MAINE WOODS

Remember thy creator in the days of thy youth. Rise free from care before the dawn, and seek adventures. Let the noon find thee by other lakes, and the night overtake thee everywhere at home. There are no larger fields than these, no worthier games than may here be played. Grow wild according to thy nature, like these sedges and brakes, which will never become English hay. Let the thunder rumble; what if it threaten ruin to farmers' crops? That is not its errand to thee. Take shelter under the cloud, while they flee to carts and sheds. Let not to get a living be thy trade, but thy sport. Enjoy the land, but own it not. Through want of enterprise and faith men are where they are, buying and selling, and spending their lives like serfs.

From WALDEN

Quaking aspen are the most widely distributed American trees, extending from coast-to-coast and into Mexico.

Time is but the stream I go a-fishing in...

The perception of beauty is a moral test.

Journal, June 21, 1852

The youth gets together his materials to build a bridge to the moon, or, perchance, a palace or temple on the earth, and, at length, the middle-aged man concludes to build a woodshed with them.

Journal, July 14, 1852

Some circumstantial evidence is very strong, as when you find a trout in the milk.

Journal, November 11, 1854

It is true, I never assisted the sun materially in his rising; but, doubt not, it was of the last importance only to be present at it.

From WALDEN

Time is but the stream I go a-fishing in. I drink at it; but while I drink I see the sandy bottom and detect how shallow it is. Its thin current slides away, but eternity remains. I would drink deeper; fish in the sky, whose bottom is pebbly with stars. I cannot count one. I know not the first letter of the alphabet. I have always been regretting that I was not as wise as the day I was born.

From WALDEN

Thoreau saw the end of his life as the sandy bottom of a stream which he compared to eternity.

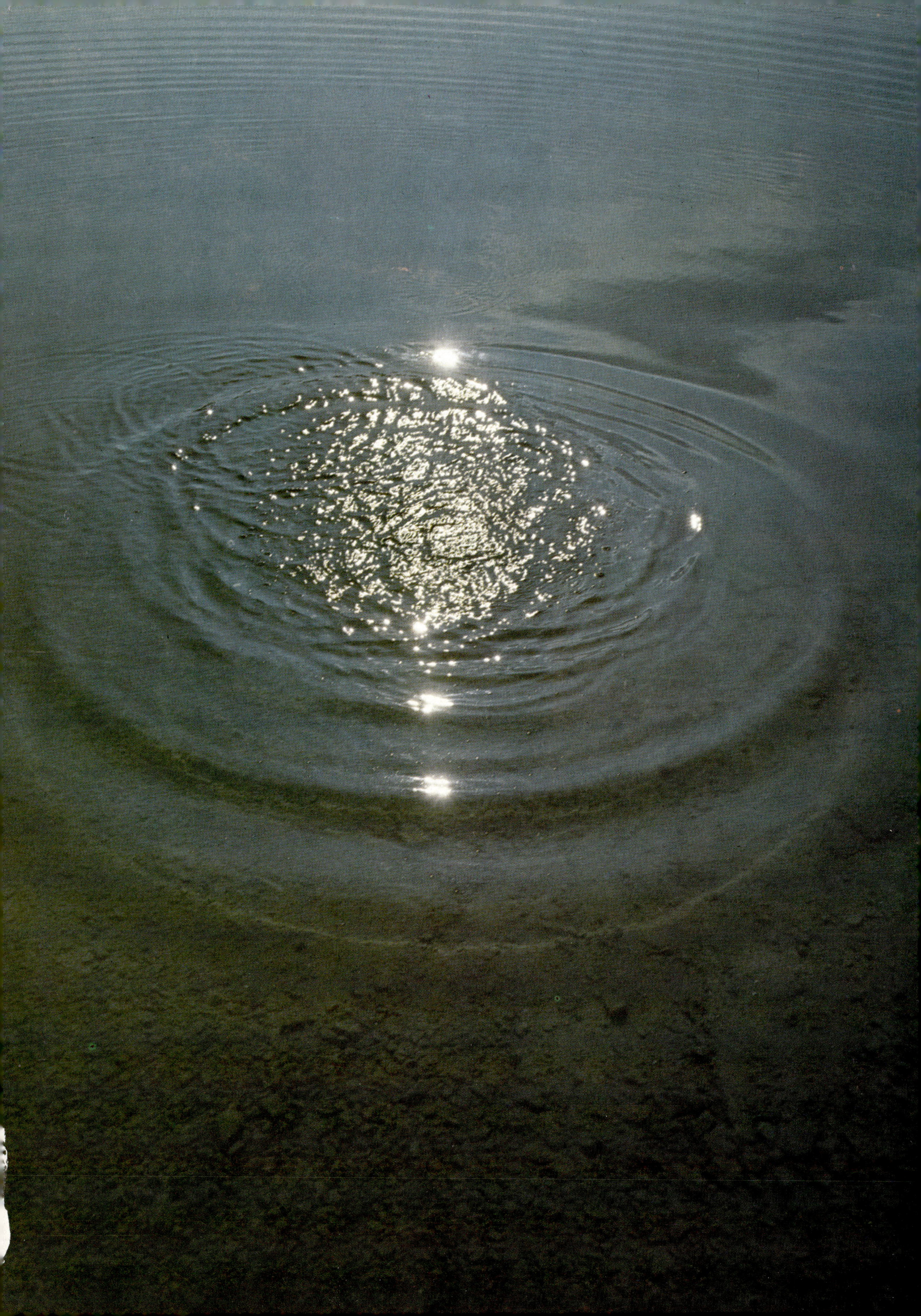

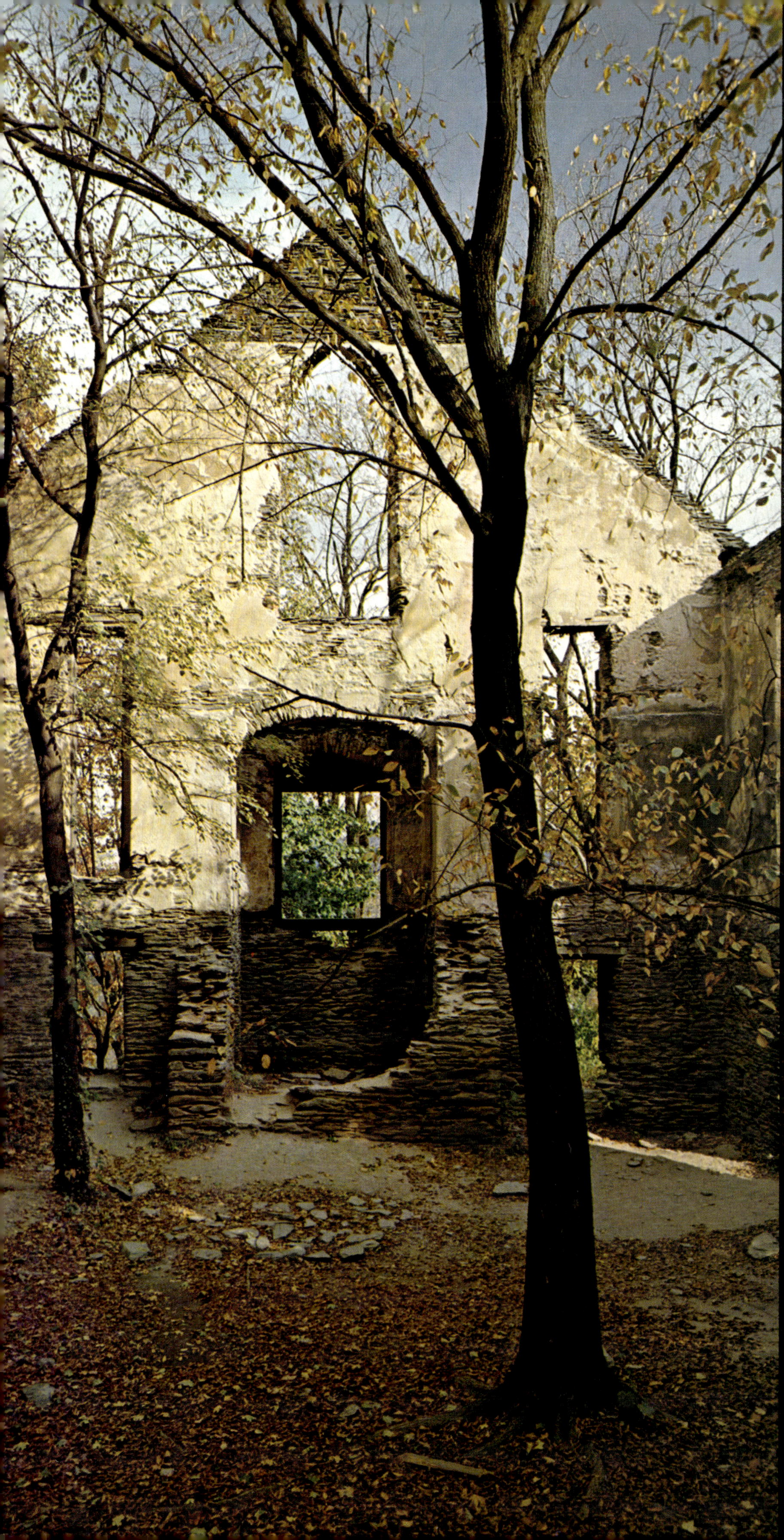
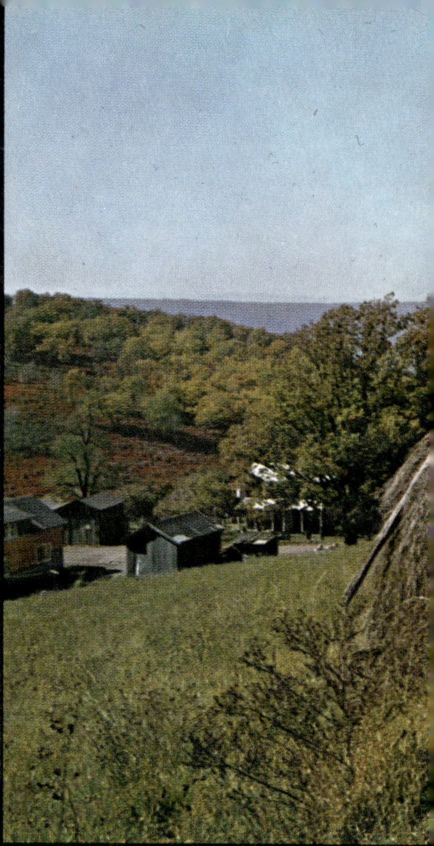
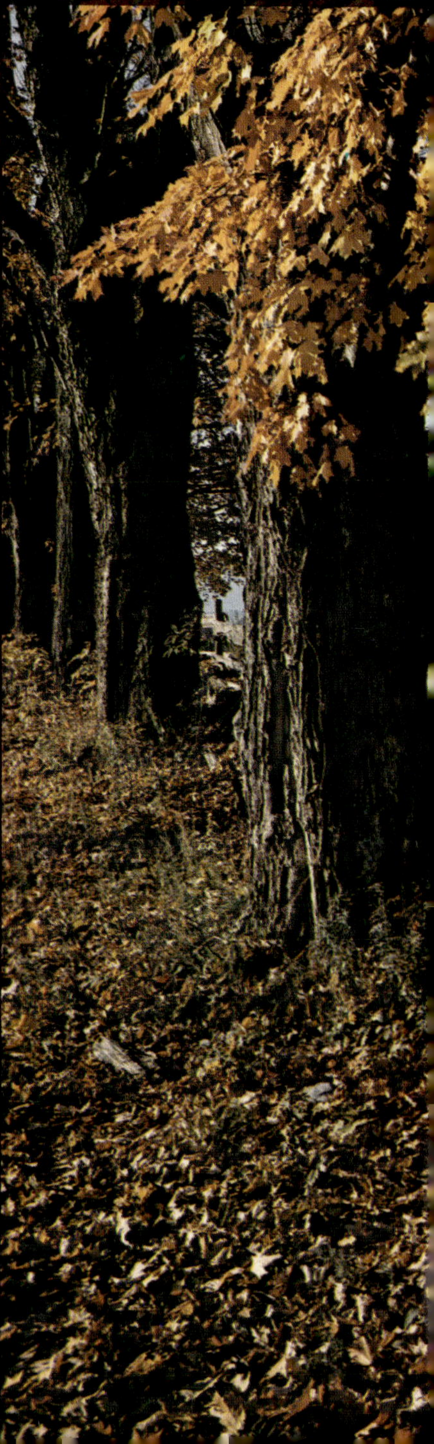

VII

THE NATURE OF MAN AND NATURE

When I go out of the house for a walk, uncertain as yet whither I will bend my steps, and submit myself to my instinct to decide for me, I find, strange and whimsical as it may seem, that I finally and inevitably settle southwest, toward some particular wood or meadow or deserted pasture or hill in that direction. My needle is slow to settle — varies a few degrees and does not always point due southwest, it is true, and it has good authority for this variation, but it always settles between west and south-southwest. The future lies that way to me, and the earth seems more unexhausted and richer on that side. . . . I turn round and round irresolute sometimes for a quarter of an hour, until I decide, for the thousandth time, that I will walk into the southwest or west. Eastward I go only by force; but westward I go free. Thither no business leads me. It is hard for me to believe that I shall find fair landscapes or sufficient wildness and freedom behind the eastern horizon. I am not excited by the prospect of a walk thither; but I believe that the forest which I see in the western horizon stretches uninterruptedly toward the setting sun, and there are no towns nor cities in it of enough consequence to disturb me. Let me live where I will, on this side is the city, on that the wilderness, and ever I am leaving the city more and more and withdrawing into the wilderness. I should not lay so much stress on this fact if I did not believe that something like this is the prevailing tendency of my countrymen. I must walk toward Oregon, and not toward Europe.

From "Walking"

June was a month of disappointment to Thoreau because summer brought an end to spring, a time of renewed optimism.

It is dry, hazy June weather. We are more of the earth, farther from heaven these days. We live in a grosser element. We [are] getting deeper into the mists of earth. Even the birds sing with less vigor and vivacity. The season of hope and promise is past; already the season of small fruits has arrived. The Indian marked the midsummer as the season when berries were ripe. We are a little saddened, because we begin to see the interval between our hopes and their fulfillment. The prospect of the heavens is taken way, and we are presented only with a few small berries. Before sundown I . . . gathered strawberries [but the] lusty strawberry plants appear to run to leaves and bear very little fruit, having spent themselves in leaves. . . .

JOURNAL, June 17, 1854

When we consider how soon some plants which spread rapidly, by seeds or roots, would cover an area equal to the surface of the globe, how soon some species of trees . . . would equal in mass the earth itself, if all their seeds became full-grown trees, how soon some fishes would fill the ocean if all their ova became full-grown fishes, we are tempted to say that every organism, whether animal or vegetable, is contending for the possession of the planet. . . . Nature opposes to this many obstacles, as climate, myriads of brute and also human foes, and of competitors which may preoccupy the ground. Each suggests an immense and wonderful greediness and tenacity of life . . . as if bent on taking entire possession of the globe wherever the climate and soil will permit. And each prevails as much as it does, because of the ample preparations it has made for the contest,—it has secured a myriad chances,—because it never depends on spontaneous generation to save it.

JOURNAL, March 22, 1861

Thoreau admired the thorough preparation each species made to complete successful reproduction.

We soon get through with Nature. She excites an expectation which she cannot satisfy. The merest child which has rambled into a copsewood dreams of a wildness so wild and strange and inexhaustible as Nature can never show him. The White Mountains . . . were smooth molehills to my expectation. We *condescend* to climb the crags of earth. . . . There was a time when the beauty and the music were all within, and I sat and listened to my thoughts, and there was a song in them. I sat for hours on rocks and wrestled with the melody which possessed me. I sat and listened by the hour to a positive though faint and distant music, not sung by any bird, nor vibrating any earthly harp. When you walked with a joy which knew not its own origin. When you were an organ of which the world was but one poor broken pipe. I lay long on the rocks, foundered like a harp on the seashore, that knows not how it is dealt with. You sat on the earth as on a raft, listening to music that was not of the earth, but which ruled and arranged it. Man *should be* the harp articulate.

JOURNAL, May 23, 1854

Overleaf: Man should attune himself to nature, Thoreau wrote, and allow her magnificence to become an inspiration to him, a magnificence which man himself should articulate to others.

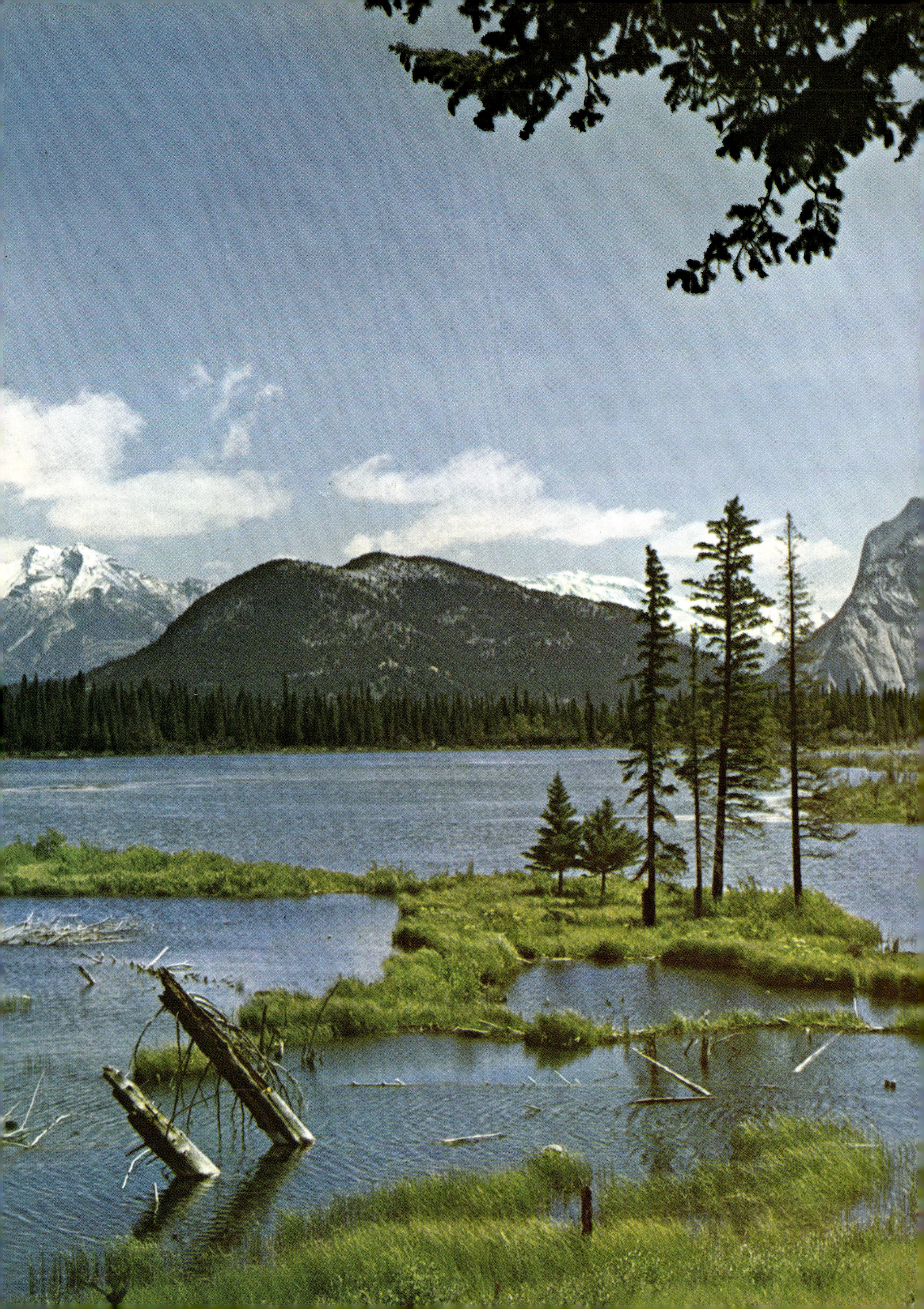

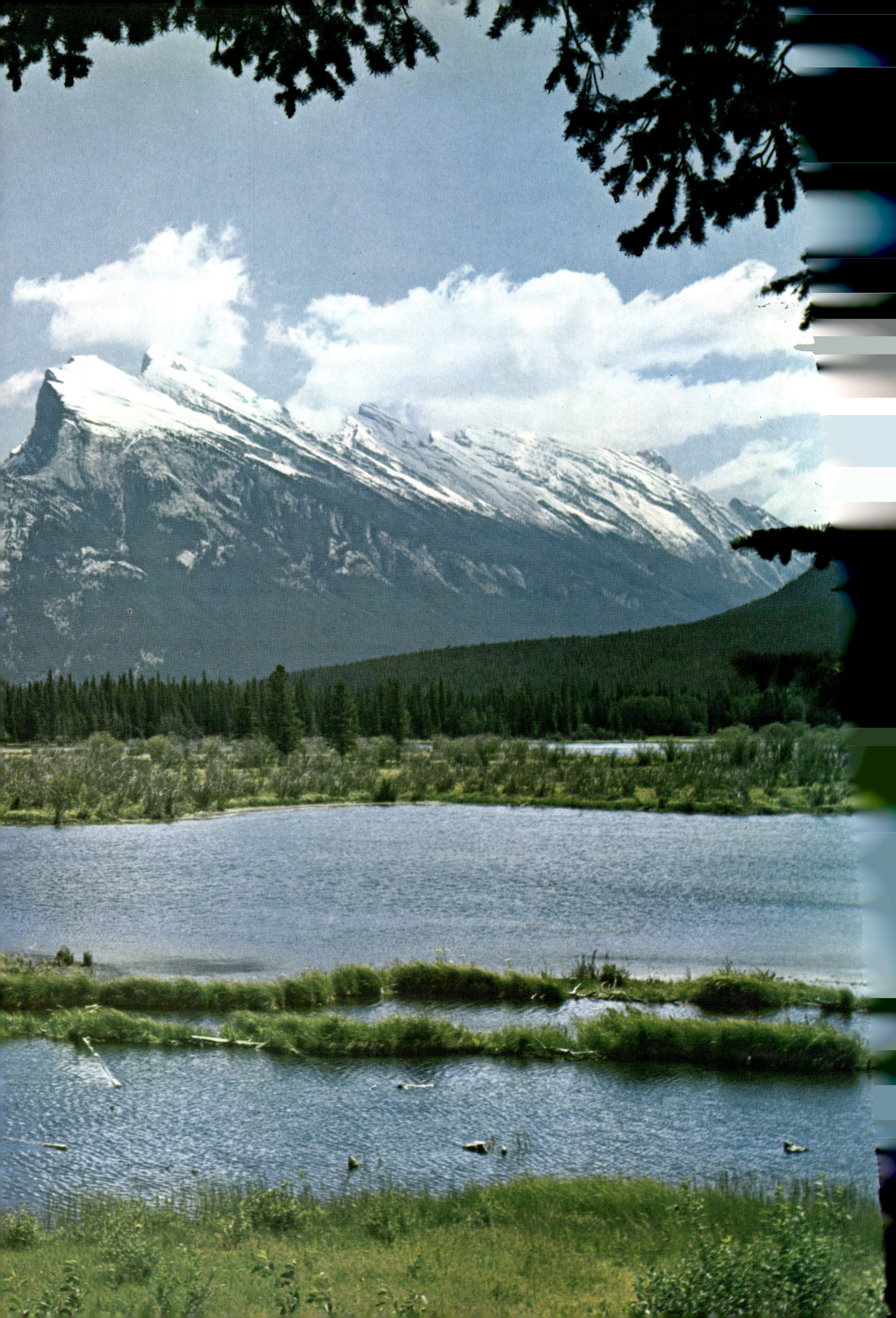

The stump serves as their monument...

A stump on a wooded hillside leading to Walden Pond near the site where Thoreau built his cabin.

I have seen many a collection of stately elms which better deserved to be represented at the General Court than the manikins beneath,— than the barroom and victualling cellar and groceries they overshadowed. When I see their magnificent domes, miles away in the horizon, over intervening valleys and forests, they suggest a village, a community, there. But, after all, it is a secondary consideration whether there are human dwellings beneath them; these may have long since passed away. I find that into my idea of the village has entered more of the elm than of the human being. They are worth many a political borough. They constitute a borough. The poor human representative of his party sent out from beneath their shade will not suggest a tithe of the dignity, the true nobleness and comprehensiveness of view, the sturdiness and independence, and serene beneficence that they do. They look from township to township. A fragment of their bark is worth the backs of all the politicians in the Union. . . . They battle with the tempests of a century. See what scars they bare, what limbs they lost before we were born! Yet they never adjourn; they steadily vote for their principles, and send their roots farther and wider from the same center. They die at their posts, and they leave a tough butt for the choppers to exercise themselves about, and a stump which serves for their monument. They attend no caucus, they make no compromise, they use no policy. Their one principle is growth. They combine a true radicalism with a true conservatism. Their radicalism is not a cutting away of roots, but an infinite multiplication and extension of them under all surrounding institutions. They take a firmer hold on the earth that they may rise higher into the heavens. . . . Their conservatism is a dead but solid heart-wood, which is the pivot and firm column of support to all this growth, appropriating nothing to itself, but forever by its support assisting to extend the area of their radicalism. Half a century after they are dead at the core, they are preserved by radical reforms. They do not, like men, from radicals turn conservatives. Their conservative part dies out first; their radical and growing part survives. They acquire new States and Territories, while the old dominions decay, and become the habitation of bears and owls and coons.

JOURNAL, January 24, 1856

The thin snow now driving from the north and lodging on my coat consists of those beautiful star crystals, not cottony and chubby spokes, as on the 13th December, but thin and partly transparent crystals. . . . How full of the creative genius is the air in which these are generated! I should hardly admire more if real stars fell and lodged on my coat. Nature is full of genius, full of the divinity; so that not a snowflake escapes its fashioning hand. . . . The same law that shapes the earth-star shapes the snow-star. . . .

What a world we live in! where myriads of these little disks, so beautiful to the most prying eye, are whirled down on every traveler's coat, the observant and the unobservant, and on the restless squirrel's fur, and on the far-stretching fields and forests, the wooded dells, and the mountain-tops. Far, far away from the haunts of man, they roll down some little slope, fall over and come to their bearings, and melt or lose their beauty in the mass, ready anon to swell some little rill with their contribution, and so, at last, the universal ocean from which they came. There they lie, like the wreck of chariot-wheels after a battle in the skies.

JOURNAL, January 5, 1856

It is difficult to conceive of a region uninhabited by man. We habitually presume his presence and influence everywhere. And yet we have not seen pure Nature, unless we have seen her thus vast and drear and inhuman, though in the midst of cities. Nature was here something savage and awful, though beautiful. I looked with awe at the ground I trod on, to see what the Powers had made there, the form and fashion and material of their work. This was that Earth of which we have heard, made out of Chaos and Old Night. Here was no man's garden, but the unhandselled globe. It was not lawn, nor pasture, nor mead, nor woodland, nor lea, nor arable, nor waste-land. It was the fresh and natural surface of the planet Earth, as it was made for ever and ever,—to be the dwelling of man, we say—so Nature made it, and man may use it if he can. Man was not to be associated with it. It was Matter, vast, terrific,—not his Mother Earth that we have heard of, not for him to tread on, or be buried in,—no, it were being too familiar even to let his bones lie there,—the home, this, of Necessity and Fate. There was there felt the presence of a force not bound to be kind to man.

From THE MAIN WOODS

This wild flower is part of the natural garden of earth, and no man has a role in its creation.

Poppies bloom amid board sidewalks and decaying buildings in an old, half-deserted town. Thoreau wrote that such an old town owes its beauty to the wild nature that makes inroads into the village.

The wilderness is near, as well as dear, to every man. Even the oldest villages are indebted to the border of wild wood which surrounds them, more than to the gardens of men. There is something indescribably inspiring and beautiful in the aspect of the forest skirting and occasionally jutting into the midst of new towns, which, like the sand-heaps of fresh fox burrows, have sprung up in their midst. The very uprightness of the pines and maples asserts the ancient rectitude and vigor of nature. Our lives need the relief of such a background, where the pine flourishes and the jay still screams.

From A WEEK ON THE CONCORD AND MERRIMACK RIVERS

It has come to this,—that the lover of art is one, and the lover of nature another, though true art is but the expression of our love of nature. It is monstrous when one cares but little about trees and much about Corinthian columns, and yet this is exceedingly common.

JOURNAL, October 9, 1857

A windy day. What have these high and roaring winds to do with the fall? No doubt they speak plainly enough to the sap that is in these trees. . . .

Ah, if I could put into words that music which I hear; that music which can bring tears to the eyes of marble statues!—to which the very muscles of men are obedient!

JOURNAL, September 28, 1852

Surely the fates are forever kind, though Nature's laws are more immutable than any despot's, yet to man's daily life they rarely seem rigid, but permit him to relax with license in summer weather. He is not harshly reminded of the things he may not do. She is very kind and liberal to all men of vicious habits, and certainly does not deny them quarter. . . .

From A WEEK ON THE CONCORD AND MERRIMACK RIVERS

Our lives are as diverse as a flowing river...

To protect his cubs the red fox never prowls areas near his den.

The life in us is like the water in the river. It may rise this year higher than man has ever known it, and flood the parched uplands; even this may be the eventful year, which will drown out all our muskrats. It was not always dry land where we dwell. I see far inland the banks which the stream anciently washed, before science began to record its freshets. Every one has heard the story which has gone the rounds of New England, of a strong and beautiful bug which came out of the dry leaf of an old table of apple-tree wood, which had stood in a farmer's kitchen for sixty years, first in Connecticut, and afterwards in Massachusetts,—from an egg deposited in the living tree many years earlier still, as appeared by counting the annual layers beyond it; which was heard gnawing out for several weeks, hatched perchance by the heat of an urn. Who does not feel his faith in a resurrection and immortality strengthened by hearing of this? Who knows what beautiful and winged life, whose egg has been buried for ages under many concentric layers of woodenness in the dead dry life of society, deposited at the first in the alburnum of the green and living tree, which has been gradually converted into the semblance of its well-seasoned tomb,—heard perchance gnawing out now for years by the astonished family of man, as they sat round the festive board,—may unexpectedly come forth from amidst society's most trivial and handselled furniture, to enjoy its perfect summer life at last!

I do not say that John or Jonathan will realize all this; but such is the character of that morrow which mere lapse of time can never make to dawn. The light which puts out our eyes is darkness to us. Only that day dawns to which we are awake. There is more day to dawn. The sun is but a morning star.

From WALDEN

Plainly the fox belongs to a different order of things from that which reigns in the village. Our courts, though they offer a bounty for his hide, and our pulpits, though they draw many a moral from his cunning, are in few senses contemporary with his free forest life.

JOURNAL, 1837-47

Thoreau compared our lives to river water because of the many possible levels between drought and flood.

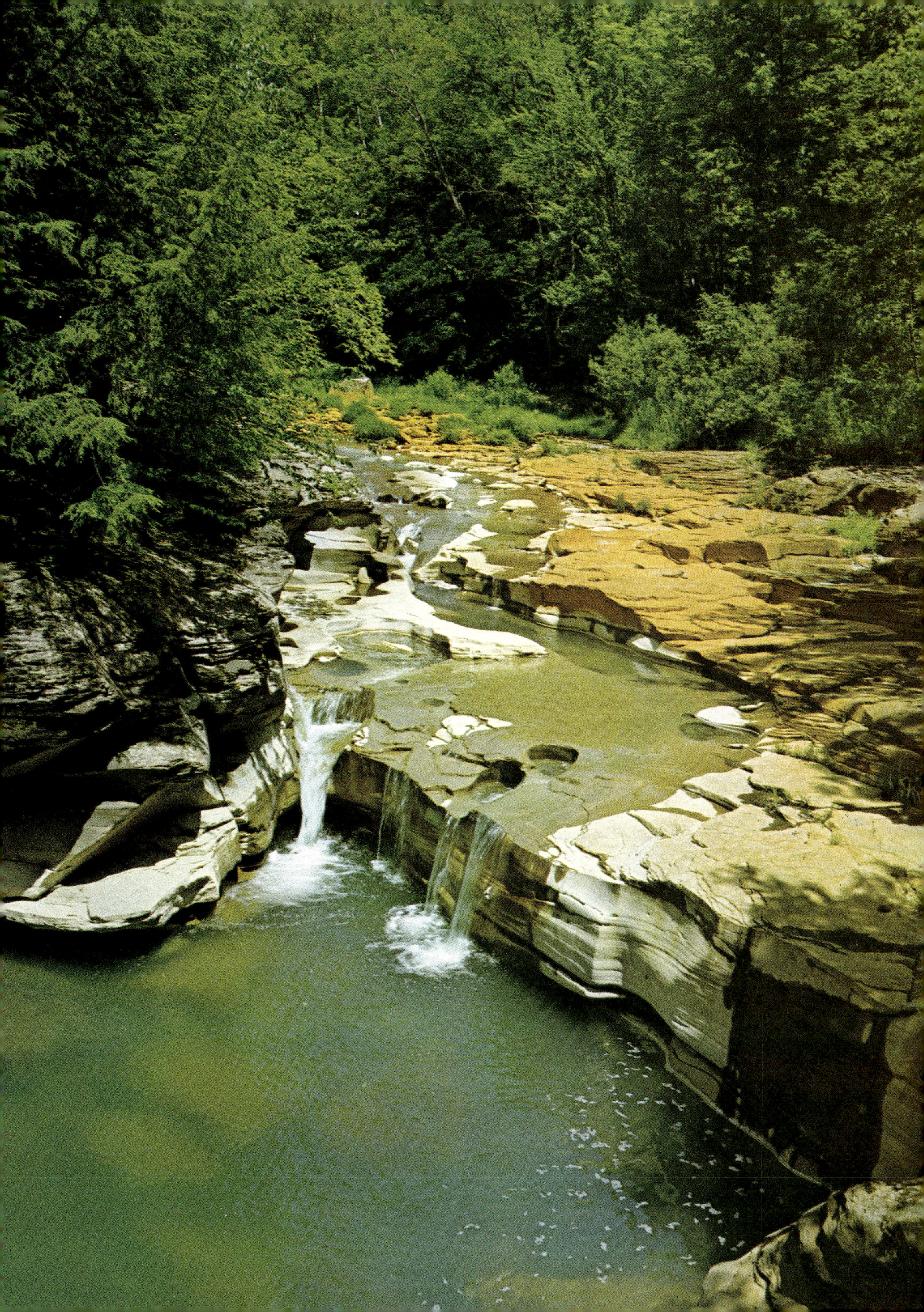

I seek to know nature, her moods and her manners...

As the afternoons grow shorter, and the early evening drives us home to complete our chores, we are reminded of the shortness of life, and become more pensive. . . . I seemed to recognize the November evening as a familiar thing come round again. . . . It appeared like a part of a panorama at which I sat spectator, a part with which I was perfectly familiar just coming into view, and I foresaw how it would look, and prepared to be pleased. . . . What new sweet was I to extract from it? . . .

It was as if I was promised the greatest novelty the world has ever seen or shall see, though the utmost possible novelty would be the difference between me and myself a year ago. This alone encouraged me, and was my fuel for the approaching winter. That we may behold the panorama with this slight improvement or change, this is what we sustain life for with so much effort from year to year.

. . . There is no more tempting novelty than this new November.

JOURNAL, November 1, 1858

I am disturbed by the sound of my steps on the frozen ground. I wish to hear the silence of the night, for the silence is something positive and to be heard. I cannot walk with my ears covered. I must stand still and listen with open ears, far from the noises of the village, that the night may make its impression on me. A fertile and eloquent silence. Sometimes the silence is merely negative, an arid and barren waste in which I shudder, where no ambrosia grows. I must hear the whispering of a myriad voices. Silence alone is worthy to be heard. Silence is of various depths and fertility, like soil. Now it is a mere Sahara, where men perish of hunger and thirst, now a fertile bottom, or prairie, of the West. As I leave the village, drawing nearer to the woods, I listen from time to time to hear the hounds of Silence baying at the Moon,—to know if they are on the track of any game. If there's no Diana in the night, what is it worth? . . . The silence rings; it is musical and thrills me. A night in which the silence was audible. I heard the unspeakable.

JOURNAL, January 21, 1853

Winter silence intrigued Thoreau. He wrote that he could hear it, that it was lyrical and thrilling.

I seek acquaintance with Nature,—to know her moods and manners. Primitive nature is the most interesting to me. I take infinite pains to know all the phenomena of spring, for instance, thinking that I have here the entire poem, and then, to my chagrin, I learn that it is but an imperfect copy that I possess and have read, that my ancestors have torn out many of the first leaves and grandest passages, and mutilated it in many places. I should not like to think that some demigod had come before me and picked out some of the best of the stars. I wish to know an entire heaven and an entire earth. All the great trees and beasts, fishes and fowl are gone. The streams, perchance, are somewhat shrunk.

Journal, March 23, 1856

Alone in distant woods or fields, in unpretending sproutlands or pastures tracked by rabbits, even in a bleak and, to most, cheerless day, like this, when a villager would be thinking of his inn, I come to myself, I once more feel myself grandly related, and that cold and solitude are friends of mine. I suppose that this value, in my case, is equivalent to what others get by church-going and prayer. I come to my solitary woodland walk as the homesick go home. I thus dispose of the superfluous and see things as they are, grand and beautiful. I have told many that I walk every day about half the daylight, but I think they do not believe it. I wish to get the Concord, the Massachusetts, the America, out of my head and be sane a part of every day.... I wish to know something; I wish to be made better. I wish to forget, a considerable part of every day, all mean, narrow, trivial men, ... and therefore I come out to these solitudes, where the problem of existence is simplified. I get away a mile or two from the town into the stillness and solitude of nature, with rocks, trees, weeds, snow about me. I enter some glade in the woods, perchance, where a few weeds and dry leaves alone lift themselves above the surface of the snow, and it is as if I had come to an open window. I see out and around myself. ... This stillness, solitude, wildness of nature is a kind of thoroughwort, or boneset, to my intellect. This is what I go out to seek. It is as if I always met in those places some grand, serene, immortal, infinitely encouraging, though invisible, companion, and walked with him.

Journal, January 7, 1857

Above: A cragged cypress tree overlooks pelicans on the rocks of the seashore.

Overleaf: Thoreau sought the solitude and silence of nature for he thought them to be a good tonic for his mind.

97

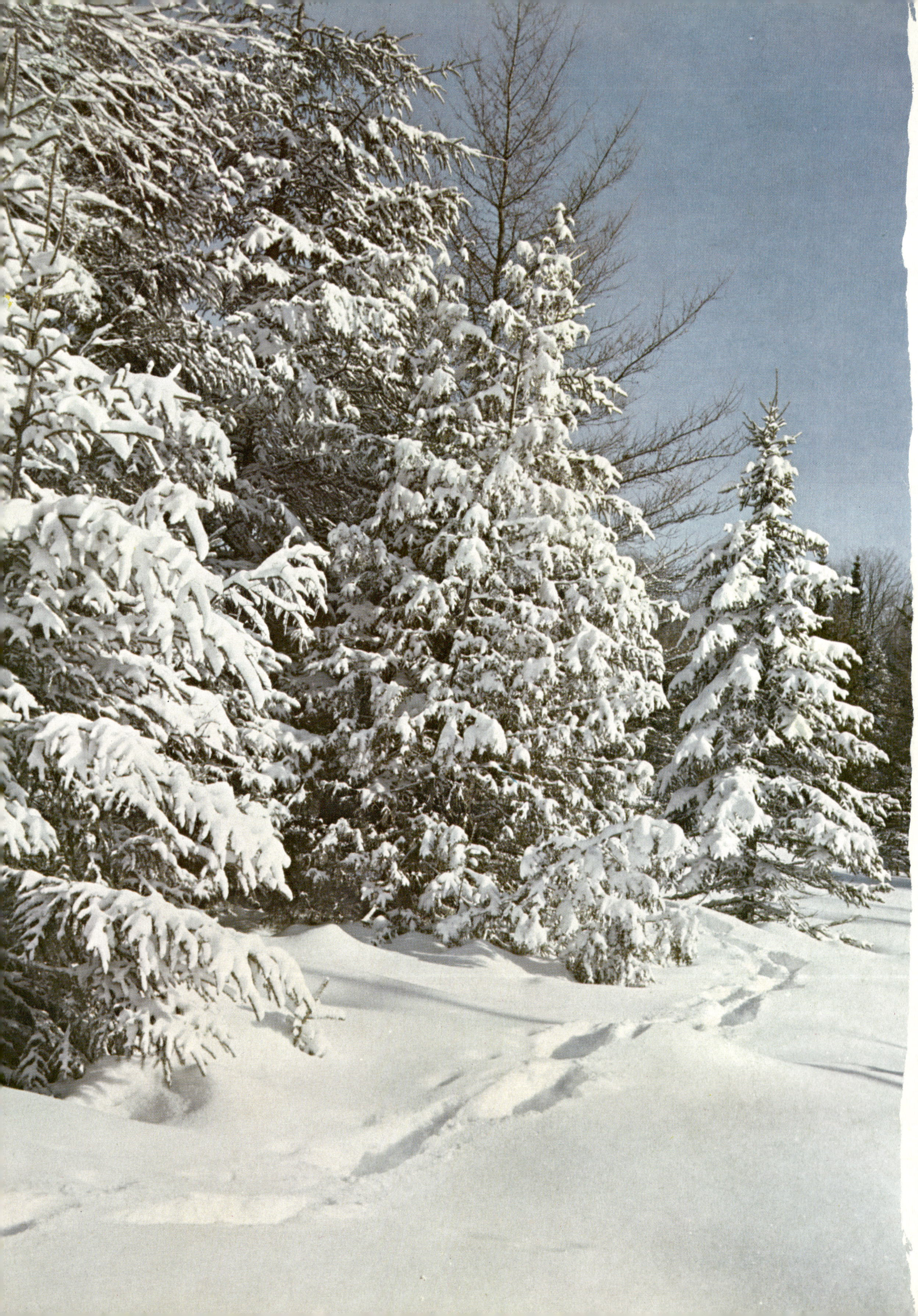